HEAD
GAMES

ALSO BY MARIAH FREDERICKS

THE TRUE MEANING OF CLEAVAGE

HEAD GAMES

Mariah Fredericks

SIMON AND SCHUSTER

SIMON AND SCHUSTER

First published in Great Britain in 2005 by Simon & Schuster UK Ltd
Africa House, 64-78 Kingsway, London WC2B 6AH
A Viacom Company.

Originally published in the USA in 2004 by Atheneum Books for Young Readers,
an imprint of Simon & Schuster Children's Division, New York.

1 3 5 7 9 10 8 6 4 2

Simon & Schuster UK Ltd
Africa House
64-78 Kingsway
London WC2B 6AH

A CIP catalogue record for this book is available from the British Library

ISBN 0 689 86053 6

Printed and bound in Great Britain by Cox & Wyman Ltd, Reading, Berkshire

For D.J.,

For letting me climb the water tower

PART ONE

GARETH

ONE

All it is, is a little pressure.

And just like that, everything changes.

You think about all the channels, all the wiring. The signal from your brain running through your nervous system to the tip of your finger. From the mouse through the cable, then . . . out there, miles and miles of electricity, snapping and crackling down the line, and then it all comes screaming right back at you.

And there it is, your answer.

Which might explain why I've been sitting here for three minutes, unable to do something as simple as bend my finger.

Just a little pressure . . .

Nope, can't do it.

I've got the cursor in place. It's right over the dice symbol, ready to give me the number.

I'm just not ready to ask for it.

I think about numbers. One through six. How much difference is there between one and six? Between two and five? Three and four? Almost none.

Out of the corner of my eye I see a new message.

Scared?

I resist the temptation to type the symbol for the finger sign.

Because I am. Scared. But he doesn't have to know that.

There has to be a connection between the noun *die* and the verb *die*. It can't be a coincidence that this little cube of chance has the same name as the ultimate bad roll.

Three is not death, I remind myself. Four is not death. Neither is five or six.

Only one and two.

I've earned a four or a five, I think. I've been playing really well.

And I've been attacked. And by someone on my team. That should earn me something, right?

But you can't earn anything in a game of chance. Luck isn't earned. It just is.

It just is.

Time to throw myself upon the mercy of the universe.

I think: Click. But my finger doesn't move.

Another message: **If you kick a dog and it doesn't move—is it dead?**

I type back: **If you kick a dog, it might jump up and bite your ass.**

I think: Things you can make happen with just a finger.

Shoot someone . . . drop the bomb . . . piss someone off. . . .

Pick your nose.

I smile.

Okay, do it now, do it now with a smile, do it with a finger up in his face, do it.

No one or two.

No one or two.

Threefourfivesix. Threefourfivesix.

I fix my eyes right on the screen. No looking away. Press.

After all that, it's easy. Just press and it's done.

Can't take it back now.

Snap, snap, screaming through the wires, the question, the answer, the request, the reward or the punishment.

What do we have for her, what do we have?

We have . . .

Four.

And I am still alive.

My mom knocks on the door, tells me it's time for dinner. I tell her, "In a minute."

She opens the door. "Judith. *Now.*"

Now I am here.

"Here" is the kitchen. "Here" is the plate on the table. Salt and pepper shakers. The mail stacked up on the counter. My mom eating.

I am here now, me again.

But the Game's still in my head. Buzzing and crackling, like in the Frankenstein movies, where they shoot the monster up with electricity.

There was a 33 percent chance I could have rolled a one or a two. If I had rolled a one or two, I would have been stuck with a very low level of strength.

Irgan, the guy who attacked me, rolled a three. But he has an extremely high level of aggression. Aggression can mean you don't need as much strength.

I can't believe he attacked.

Can't believe I actually survived. . . .

My mom says, "You sit too close to the screen."

My mom—the other person at the table obsessed with the Game.

"It's really not good for your eyes," she says.

I nod over my plate.

"You think I'm nagging, but I'm not."

I smile. "No, I know."

But she is. Nagging. The problem is not the screen. Or my eyes.

My mom just hates the Game.

She sighs dramatically. "I remember when people used to play games with other people."

"I do play with other people," I remind her.

"I mean people you can see. People who are there."

"They are there," I say patiently. "They just happen to be in other places while they're there."

Like Timbuktu. Or Anchorage. Or Third Avenue.

Now, if I had rolled a three . . .

My mom's voice. "Do you know anything about these people? Who they are?"

"What does it matter?"

"It does matter," she says. "It matters because there are sick people out there."

Mom's biggest fear. Perverts on the Internet.

It's a joke. The new bogeyman.

I should make a joke, actually. Something about monsters under the bed.

But for some reason my throat's tight—whatever I say, it'll come out wrong. It's the images in my mother's head. Drooling old men reaching out to put their hands on you. Their gross, sticky fingers. *Come here, little girl.*

Joke. Think of a joke.

I grin. "Well, then it's definitely a good thing that there's a lot of distance between me and them."

"And you'll keep it that way?" She's all intense. "Someone asks to meet you, you say no?"

"I say no."

For a few minutes we eat. My mom tries to decide if she's satisfied, while I try to be as small as possible, give her no target. I know we're both thinking, Why do we have to fight about this? Except my mom's also thinking, If only she'd quit, and I'm thinking, If only *she'd* quit.

My mom is not the worst. She tries. Only sometimes too hard.

Then from the outside hallway we hear the rumble of the elevator, someone getting off on our floor. Our kitchen's right by the front door, so you can hear everyone coming and going.

Well, you can hear the Heitmans. They're the only other family that lives on our hall.

My mom pretends to be eating. But I can tell she's listening. Trying to figure out: Is it Mrs. Heitman? Mr. Heitman? Or Jonathan?

It's almost nine o'clock. It could be Mrs. Heitman coming home from work.

It can't be Mr. Heitman coming home from work. Mr. Heitman doesn't have a job.

Could be Jonathan. Coming home from wherever.

The door to the Heitmans' apartment opens. Closes.

My mom waits a second, then says in a low voice, "I saw her the other day."

"Who? Mrs. Heitman?"

My mom nods. "She looked completely exhausted."

I shake my head and Mom shakes hers, too. We may not agree on the Game, but we do agree about Mrs. Heitman. We feel bad for her. And we like her. Even though we don't know her that well.

We should, when you think about it. Know her better.

The Heitmans have lived next door as long as we've been here—practically forever.

But the Heitmans aren't really the kind of people you know. They're the kind of people you stay away from. Not Mrs. H., but Mr. Heitman sort of. And Jonathan *definitely*.

My mom reaches across the table and squeezes my hand. Like, *Maybe my kid spends too much time on the computer, but she's not a psycho like Jonathan Heitman.*

Then she gives me a big smile. "Hey, when's Leia coming around? I miss that girl."

I take a drink of soda. I wish there were a way, when you don't ever want to think about somebody again, that you could erase the memory of their existence from other people's minds. Because as long as they're in someone's head, they exist. Which means you end up talking about them.

Which means you have to remember they exist.

"I mean, now that the school year's started, and you guys are back at Connolly, I'm assuming you'll be as inseparable as ever."

Lie or tell the truth?

I can't decide, so I end up not saying anything.

"How was her summer?" My mom's still on it.

I concentrate on my plate. "I don't really know."

"You don't know?"

"No."

My mom frowns, then asks, "What? You guys have a fight?"

"No, we just . . ." I shrug. "I don't know."

She waits for a second, then says, "Well, whatever it is, I can't imagine you won't work it out."

I nod. Because I don't know what else to say.

"Maybe you should give her a call."

"Yeah, I *did*." That comes out wrong, and I start forking up carrots.

It's a weird thing: When you get loud, everyone else gets quiet. I can feel my mom dying to ask, "So? What happened?"

But instead she changes the subject. And I let her.

Because she's right. She really doesn't want to know.

Later, as I wash the dishes, I think about aggression. When someone attacks and they're stronger than you . . .

Way more aggressive than you . . .

How do you fight back? How do you win?

What can you use to defend yourself?

Intelligence, for one thing. Weaponry, obviously.

Luck.

I'm not sure if I have luck or not.

In fact, I'm fairly sure I don't.

You can always start over, I tell myself. It is only a game.

Only it's not.

TWO

My great-uncle Albert was called Crazy Uncle Albert because he was a genius. At least, people thought he was a genius because he was good at math, and no one could figure out how his mind worked. Actually, it didn't work a lot of the time. There were basic life things he couldn't do, like drive a car or talk to people.

But his mind worked really well when it came to numbers. So well that during World War II the government sent him to Los Alamos to work on the bomb. After the war he taught at a college. But then he just kind of lost whatever normal mind he had and became a hermit somewhere until he died.

We have one picture of him. He's your classic dork. High-water pants, glasses, weird crew-cut hair. He's standing in some field with his shoulders back, like someone told him, "Pose for the camera." I guess he meant to stick out his chest, but the first thing you see is his stomach.

He looks like a nice person, though. He's got this big smile, like he's thrilled someone would want to take his picture.

My mom says I'm like him. She says that's where I get my "math mind."

I don't *look* like him, and I hate to be mean, but I'm a little glad about that. Not that I would say this to Mom about her uncle, but . . . no harm in thinking it.

My dad said that to me a few years ago: "There's no harm in thinking." We were talking about Crazy Uncle Albert and whether it was right to use your brain to build weapons.

He said, "You can't expect people not to think. Not to know things just because they *could* be bad."

I said, "Yeah, but then they built it and a hundred thousand people died."

My dad laughed and said there were a lot of steps between the thinking and doing.

Which I know, duh. All I was saying is that when you think of doing something, you don't always know the consequences. For a while people *thought* about building the bomb, but nothing happened. In the end it was a lot of different people doing a lot of different things, most of which had nothing to do with the bomb, that did make it happen.

I think about that sometimes. Who was the person who had the first thought, the one that started it all?

And after they had the thought, what was the first thing they did?

I know my uncle never thought, Hey, all this great science—one day I'll use it to kill a whole bunch of people. You just look at his picture; he's not that kind of guy.

And yet, I guess in a way he sort of is.

On the next page of the scrapbook there's a picture of my dad. He's a little kid, standing in a yard in front of a big house. That's just one picture of him; obviously we have more. Him and my mom, him and me. But nothing for the last five years. Not since he moved to Seattle, where he got a job at a university.

I used to think of my dad and think of a smell. His sweaters had this rough, woolly smell, and when you hugged him, you just breathed it in.

Now I think of a voice, "Hey, kiddo." Which is usually the first thing he says when he calls. He calls me every week.

Sometimes when I talk to him on the phone, I try to picture him in his house talking to me. If he's sitting down or walking around. Doodling.

And sometimes I think maybe he isn't in his house. Maybe he's in his car, or another state. Or another part of the world. Maybe this is just a tape.

13

That's when I say something bizarre like, "I thought I saw a lizard on the crosstown bus the other day," something no computer could think of a response to.

Just to make sure.

Right now all I'm thinking of doing is raising my hand.

Action: Raise hand in math class.

Consequence: Get answer wrong. Look like complete moron.

I think I'll keep my hand down.

It's easy to look like a moron in this class. It's full of extremely smart people. Because I'm here, I'm supposed to be one of them, but I can't help feeling someone made a big mistake. And that any second now Mr. Jarman, the teacher, is going to figure that out.

On the very first day he said, "I expect you all to participate. That means speaking up, taking part. Anybody who thinks this class is about tests and homework is wrong. Math is dynamic. Math is about risk. You can't be afraid to be *wrong*—even in front of your classmates."

That's really when I should have raised my hand. *Uh, Mr. Jarman? Sorry. I don't do those things.*

Because all that sounds great, right? But the thing is, at Connolly everyone is hypercompetitive. About everything. Money. Looks. But mostly intelligence. If you're at Connolly, you're supposed to be smart. Like . . . the best. Whatever that means. Kids who are in the top ten of the class want to be in the top three. Kids in the top three want to be number one. I don't know what number one wants to be. Probably a professor at MIT.

So if you get something wrong in front of your classmates, it's not like they're going to go, "Oh, that's really interesting, let's talk about that." They're going to go, "Ha, ha, you suck."

Be invisible—that's my solution. Do my thing, but basically, if no one knows you exist, no one's going to try and come after you. I'm not a star, one of those kids on Mathletes or a statewide prize winner—and I want to keep it that way.

Now Jarman's prowling around the classroom, waiting for an answer.

I really should raise my hand. Get it over with. It's the second week of school, and practically everyone's had their hand up at least once but me.

I'm pretty sure I know the answer.

So, just raise your stupid hand.

Maybe I'm paralyzed. Because my brain is telling my hand to move, but my hand's not listening.

Perhaps it knows my brain doesn't mean it.

Raise your hand!

I lift my fingers off the table. But just as I'm thinking, Rise, Sir Wrist, Peter Nardo's hand shoots up, and Jarman shouts, "Yes, Peter!"

Great. Peter Nardo was the only other person in class who hadn't said anything yet.

Now I'm the only one left.

I get through the rest of class okay. But as I get up to leave I can feel Mr. Jarman watching me.

You're next.

One day I'm going to invent a game called *Lunchroom*.

Lunchroom: Where no one survives.

You could have evil counter ladies, toxic food, spaghetti sauce spills that make you stick to the floor. The line that NEVER ENDS! The vending machine that EATS YOUR MONEY! The foul stench that KNOCKS YOU UNCONSCIOUS!

Your challenge is to make it through the crowd and find a safe place. Various things can kill you, from putrid veggie burgers to the explosion of laughter that occurs right after you drop your lunch tray. And every person you see, you have to figure out friend or foe, threat level, potential for alliance, and so on.

Like right now, coming at me is Ray Girardi. Won't hurt, won't help. He's a neutral.

But on my left is a table I call the Isle des Snobs. They can freeze you if you get too close. Avoid at all costs. Next to them is the Mathlete crowd. They look like potential allies, but they're all in Jarman's class and have an interest in wiping you out as a threat. Assess risk. Decide not worth it.

Allies are almost never worth the risk.

I spot an empty table in the far corner. It's right by the vending machine, which is why no one wants it. But it's perfect for me.

One problem: I have to pass by Leia to get there.

The ex-friend who GIVES YOU THE LOOK OF DEATH!

And Leia is not alone. Leia has allies.

Namely, her new best friends, Kelsey and Jessica.

It's funny, until the end of last year Leia never even mentioned K&J. They were completely off her radar. But this year you'd think they'd all been buds since first grade. They do everything together. Lunch. After school. They even tried to get the same classes.

They laugh the same way too, at the same time. Then they laugh about how they laugh.

And to get to my safe place, the gross, sticky table by the vending machine, I have to walk past all three of them.

Okay. The thing to do is pretend complete ignorance of their existence. Like my mom says about people I play the Game with: "You don't see them, so how can they possibly exist?"

Also, do not breathe while passing by them. Ex-friends can emit poisonous gases.

Basically, be invisible.

They do see me—I know because they stop giggling for two whole seconds—but they pretend not to. No snickers, no nasty comments. This time, anyway.

Maybe Leia thinks I have a high threat potential.

Yeah, right. She just refuses to acknowledge that you exist.

Well, same here.

Finally I reach the table, where I pull out my Game notebook. In it I keep a record of my moves and the moves of certain other players. It helps me strategize. Also, to ignore people.

As I look over my notes from yesterday's game I keep thinking about how my mom's always worried some creep from the Game will hunt me down and kill me.

And now someone *is* trying to kill me.

I don't get it. What does Irgan the Head Case want with me?

There's a burst of laughter, mean laughter; some poor soul just got zapped. Even I look up to see who it is, and that's when I see Katie Mitchell standing at the outer edge of the tables, her tray tilted, a huge splash of soda on the floor next to her.

Katie. Of course.

In *Lunchroom: The Game* definitely one of the weakest levels of player would be a Katie. The fat, rich girl who tries too hard to get people to like her, so of course nobody does. Katie's a total airhead. Airheads don't do well at Connolly.

Everybody says about Katie that her parents got her into Connolly because they gave a lot of money to the school. Which is a horrible thing to say about anybody, but she's such a dip you kind of believe it.

Right now she's faced with that most dire of *Lunchroom* scenarios: nowhere to sit.

18

Last year she could have sat with Kelsey and Jessica. They were her "friends" last year, even though K&J made it clear that Katie should feel honored that they let her hang with them. I guess she agreed, because she never seemed to mind how they put her down.

Then at the end of last year Leia started hanging around with Kelsey and Jessica. Guess who was odd girl out?

As Katie wanders around looking for somewhere, anywhere, to sit, she glances over at Leia and K&J, but they totally ignore her.

I'm about to go back to my notebook, when Katie looks over, sees me watching her, and breaks into this huge grin.

Oh no, I think. No, no, no . . .

Too late. Katie's headed this way.

"Hey, mind if I sit down?" She doesn't wait to hear yes, just sits. "Being Psycho Student Woman, I see." She nods at my notebook. "God, I haven't even, like, *started*. I think my brain is still on vacation. What brain I actually have."

This is how Katie talks. Nonstop. Like if she stops for air, you'll tell her to get lost.

I have no choice. I put the notebook back in my bag. So weak I can't even defend myself against Katie Mitchell.

"So, what's up?" Katie smiles and bites her lip at the same time. "You have a cool summer?"

"Yeah, pretty cool."

"I went to Maui."

"Whoa." Which, I think, is the right thing to say.

"Yeah, kind of sucks if you're not Bikini Goddess, but hey. Decent shopping."

She nods. So I nod. And think, Katie, what are you doing here?

But I know what she's doing here. I don't even have to look at Leia and her pals snickering to know.

Katie glances back at where they're mopping up her soda spill. "Could you believe I did that? God, I am, like, Klutz Woman today."

I say, "I've done it a hundred times." I haven't, but why be a jerk?

"I probably ruined my shoes." She looks down, all upset.

Okay, that's it. Maui is one thing. Shopping and Maui—maybe okay. But I am not going to listen to shopping, Maui, and shoes just so Katie has someone to sit with at lunch. Just so she can pretend she has a new "best friend," and hasn't been totally dissed by K&J.

I start getting up. "You know, I have to go. I've got this huge test coming up."

Katie nods. Like she totally expected to get blown off. "Sure. Hey, maybe I'll see you around."

I nod back. Escape, escape . . .

Of course, I don't have a test. No one does the second week of school.

But I do have a psycho killer on my butt, and if I don't figure out how to get rid of him, I may be dead in four hours.

■□■□

Three thirty. One hour to Game time.

From Connolly to my house it's twenty-three blocks. Twenty down and three across.

Last year I always walked the same way.

And I still go the same way this year.

Which means walking past 158 West Seventy-first Street.

Some numbers are ill omened. They have their own particular energy. You can actually feel it sometimes when you come across them. It's heavy, oppressive. Like the feeling in the air right before a storm.

With 158 West Seventy-first Street it's something about the combination of numbers. They feel out of sync. Nothing quite fits with anything else and nothing wants to. There's all kinds of cracks and fissures in the surface. It's not a solid gateway. A lot can get through.

Sometimes, in order to make my way past it, I tell myself it's just a door. It's green, it's got gold numbers on it—158. That's all it is, just a door.

I remind myself that it's daytime. Broad daylight. Everyone can see everything.

Ill-omened things can work *for* you, I tell myself. It's not a bad thing to come in contact with a destructive force, absorb some of its power.

Still, I hate walking on Seventy-first Street.

Leia Taplow lives on Seventy-first Street.

But that's not why.

It doesn't matter why.

Today I walk right by it without looking. But I know when it's coming, and right before, I feel myself speed up, walk just a little faster.

I hate myself for that.

Tomorrow I'll do it again, exactly the same way. Only I won't run.

I glance at my watch. Start walking faster.

Almost Game time.

THREE

Last year for social studies I had to write an essay called "Where I Live." You could make it anywhere you wanted. Like some kids wrote about the planet, and other kids wrote about their bedroom. I wrote about my building, which is the Bradnor, on Ninety-first Street.

Maybe seventy families live here. Everybody knows each other.

Well, at least something about each other.

Like everybody knows that Mrs. Levine in 1C has twenty-four cats in her apartment, but she tells the building she has only two.

Everybody knows that the Caldwells in 4E fight all the

time because he's an opera singer and she drinks too much.

Everybody knows that Mr. Heitman in 12B was fired a year ago and hasn't found a job yet. And that Mrs. Heitman works two jobs to keep Jonathan in some school for screwups after he got thrown out of the last one.

Obviously I didn't put that in my essay. But I did think how strange it is. The way, without even knowing it, people leave little pieces of their lives floating around. You look at those little bits and you think, Okay, that's them. That's who they are. Like, I don't know what Mrs. Levine thinks about herself, but to me she's Mrs. Levine in 1C with the cats.

Here's what the building knows about Jonathan Heitman.

A few years ago a kid from our building got caught shoplifting. When his parents checked his room, they found tons of stolen stuff: CDs, candy, even video games. The kid freaked and told them Jonathan had made him do it. At first it'd been fun, like a game. But then Jonathan told him he'd rat him out unless he stole a certain amount every week.

They know he does drugs. Mr. Dalmas, the janitor, found some drug stuff in the basement, and everyone says it has to be Jonathan's.

They know he broke into the coin box on the washing machines in the laundry room. At least, they're pretty sure it was him. "He's a druggie," I heard Mrs. Rosen say. "Druggies steal."

The building knows a lot about Jonathan. He leaves a lot of himself around.

In fact, he's kind of splattered all over the place.

In the elevator I press the button for twelve.

If you look lower, you'll see the button for the sixth floor. It's black. Hard plastic.

Someone's scratched a swastika on it.

Here's something the building doesn't know about Jonathan Heitman.

It was over the summer. I don't remember where I was going—only that when I walked out of my apartment, there he was.

That almost never happens: me being alone with Jonathan. We live in totally different time zones. Not to mention universes.

He did say, "Hey." But I didn't say anything back; I figured anything I said would sound stupid to him.

When the elevator finally came, I let him go in first. He slouched in the corner. I stayed as close to the door as possible. Not that I was afraid of him or anything. But there's always been something about him, you don't want to get too close.

I pressed for the ground floor. And that's when I saw it. The button.

Without thinking, I said, "That's really ill."

I looked over at him. He shrugged, a little smile on his face. And I knew he had done it.

I looked back at the button, so ugly and so . . . dumb. Like, *Nyah, nyah. Can't get me.*

I said, "Some people in the building lived through that. It's not a joke."

He rolled his eyes. "It's a total joke."

I stared at the door, watched the floors disappear. Because I didn't know what else to say. Like Jonathan had taken everything that was real and decided that because it didn't mean anything to him, it couldn't mean anything to anyone else.

Someone else, I thought, would know exactly what to say. They would know the exact right words to make Jonathan feel small and stupid, which is what he deserves to feel.

I was really pissed off at myself that I wasn't one of those people.

It bugged me for weeks. I couldn't get over what a wimp I'd been. But then I realized that's what Jonathan gets off on.

Making people feel helpless.

Nobody's home at my house. The whole place has a silent, deserted feel.

I love this time of day.

I go to my room, shut the door, and sit down at my desk.

I plug the line into the phone.

Tap space bar, go to Favorites.

There it is. The Game.

The funny thing about the Game is I haven't been doing it that long. Not even a year.

I guess I seriously got into it over the summer. Last year I was in this bookstore, and somehow I ended up in the gaming section, where I saw this book called *Hell's Mouth: The Guide*. And I was like, What? Because Hell's Mouth was this weird, out-there fantasy series that I'd read a million years ago.

But what they had done was take the world of Hell's Mouth and made it a setting for a game. This universe where you could tell any story you wanted, be anyone you wanted.

I don't know why I bought it. It wasn't like I had anyone to play with.

Then over the summer I saw they had this online version. And I thought, Why not?

It's weird when you find something that totally fits you. Something that tells you so much about who you are. You can't really believe it wasn't always there somehow in your brain.

Although, who knows how much longer I'll be playing. At least with this group.

Up until now all the groups I played with had a strict policy: You do not attack your fellow players. Mad slashers need not apply.

That's not how it is with this group.

They did warn me. When I joined, Figuroa9, the game master, said, "Control is minimal."

But I thought, Okay, what's that like?

I guess now I know.

Hey! Here!—Ola

Fester lurking.—Fester

God, again? You'll go blind.—Terryn

Fester should know I'm kidding. He's a good guy.

You wish. Dirty rotten thief.—Fester

I smile, then type: **Pretty good thief, thank you.**—Terryn

There's a little pause. Then: **Maybe too good. I wasn't sure who to root for in your little scrap with the Head Case.**—Fester

Before I can respond, Ola writes, **Zero tolerance for mad slashers!**

Mad slasher. Someone who's just into the Game for the pleasure of killing. Irgan the Head Case says he's not. . . .

But the fact is, we used to be six players. Now we're only five.

It used to be me, Ola, Fester, J-Boy, Irgan, and this guy named Verger.

Then a month ago Irgan put his sword through Verger's skull.

Now, it's true that Verger was a whiny jerk. But we were all surprised when Figuroa9, the game master, ruled it an acceptable move. At the time I thought, Well, they did warn us. Control is minimal.

But then last week Irgan came after me.

In the Game we're officially working together on a mission to find the exiled ruler of Hazird.

But unofficially I have a new mission: Survive Irgan.

Which is why today's goal is to get a better shield.

My character is a thief. My strengths are stealth, deception, speed. I rely on not being noticed, not getting caught. And a certain level of diplomacy, which means the ability to talk your way out of trouble.

That's not enough when facing superior aggression and strength.

Death is not death. It just means you're out of the Game.

And it is only a game, I remind myself.

All of a sudden a message appears and I jump.

Shall we begin?—Figuroa9

Almost immediately I'm in trouble.

Ola has a shield she can sell me. But she's inside the tavern, and I have to meet her there.

Frankly, I should have the shield *before* I go in the tavern because it's a rough and ugly place. But I don't really have a choice.

As I approach the tavern a message comes up. **Irgan catches sight of Terryn getting ready to rob the tavern. Moves to intercept, as robbery may jeopardize the mission.**

It's a very strange moment. When someone tells you that they want to harm you. When you understand that

29

you're not crazy. You're not paranoid. There are malign forces out there. People of ill will.

And the only question left is, What are you going to do?

It'd be nice if Figuroa9 stepped in. *Bzzz! Illogical move!*

But nothing. Silence.

While the other players make their moves, I assess. I'm threatened on two sides. Irgan in back of me, tavern in front of me. Of all the players only Ola is near enough to be any help.

A thief and a witch. Against a seven-foot psychopath with a sword. Yeah, that's going to work.

What do I have? What can I fight with?

A sword, but no shield. Not much help when your physical strength is level four and your opponent's is eight.

One lousy spell. I do have that. But it's not very strong. . . .

It's Ola's move. She writes: **Ola leaves the tavern.**

She's trying to help me. Come outside so I don't have to go inside the tavern. I want to type, "Ola, you rule."

But then a message pops up. **Makes no sense. How does Ola know Terryn is outside?**—Figuroa9

Which means Ola has to stay put.

I think: What is your deal, Figuroa9? Why are you helping Irgan?

My move.

Irgan's too close. I don't have a choice. Somehow I have to confront him. I can try one of two things. Diplomacy—or intimidation.

Let's try diplomacy.

I type: **First I'm picking your pocket. Now my ambitions have risen to the entire tavern. Why don't we go inside together? First round's on me.**—Terryn

Message from Figuroa9: **Diplomacy works only if the other party is willing to listen. You'll have to try intimidation.**

I roll, but not even a six will help me intimidate Irgan. When I get a two, I hardly even feel it.

Irgan's move.

For a long time the screen is blank. I have to remind myself to breathe. It's only words on a screen.

He could accept my offer. He does have that choice.

Or he could cut me into a million pieces.

But I can't believe they wouldn't toss him out of the Game if he did.

Okay, Irgan, what are you going to do?

This waiting is driving me nuts. Let him get it over already.

I type: **Scared?**

Because that's what he asked me last game.

Then I see on the screen: **Irgan draws his sword. Advances on Terryn.**

Guess that answers that question.

Irgan has to roll for the accuracy of his first blow. Given his strength, anything above one and I'm screwed.

Irgan rolls a one. A clear miss.

For once I'm lucky.

At least, until Irgan's next move.

One by one the players make their moves. Fester and J-Boy are too far away from the scene to be of any use; Ola's been warned once. I'm on my own here.

Thanks, Figuroa9. Much appreciated.

Here are my choices: Stay here, get slaughtered by Irgan. Go into the tavern, get slaughtered by the thugs in there.

What can you use against superior strength and aggression?

Sword and spell. Sword and spell.

Spell . . .

I glance at my notebook. Irgan's physical strength is eight. Mine's only four. But my powers of concentration are much, much higher. Ten to his three. Spells are tricky in combat. I need a roll of four or better to make it happen.

I think: This is not going to work.

But nothing else will work either, so why not try this?

I type: **They say you must be very brave or very foolish to cast a spell in combat. I would say a touch of madness helps.**

I roll. . . .

Six.

I throw the spell. Irgan is frozen.

And for my next move I take his shield.

Because, hey, that's what a thief would do.

After the game I sit for a while. Sometimes life is good and you just have to let it be.

Then I decide it's enough, time to shut down. Before I do, I check my e-mail. And see . . .

Greetings!—Figuroa9

He's never e-mailed me before. My first impulse is, Delete. Screw him, the guy ruled against me the entire game.

But it could be Game business. Scheduling or something like that.

Besides, I'm curious.

I know nothing about Figuroa9. Who he is. Or even if he is a he.

I wonder what he thinks I play like. If he knows I'm a she.

I click on the message. It reads: **Just wanted to congratulate you on the excellent move against Irgan. He's been asking for it. Definitely the highlight of today's game!**

Which is cool. But weird. I feel like someone touched me, and I don't like that. Figuroa9 sounds different in this e-mail than in the Game. You can tell he has a Game voice and a normal one.

And now I feel like I have to write back. In my "normal" voice.

I mean, I don't have to. But it'd be nice if Figuroa9 were on my side the next time Irgan attacks.

Because there will be a next time.

I could be really short, to the point. Just: "Thanks."

But that doesn't seem like enough. It sounds like, *Yes, I am a gaming goddess. All praise and worship me.*

Maybe "Thanks" and something about combining business and pleasure.

No, keep pleasure out of it.

Quickly I hit Reply. Type: **Thanks. He did have it coming (tho will admit serious need for armor). Isn't there a way. . . .**

No, delete. "Isn't there a way" is too singsong, too girlie. *Gosh, Mr. Man, isn't there a way?*

I wish we could . . . No, gone.

"Irgan in permanent exile"? Yeah, that's okay. "I'm liking the vision of Irgan in permanent exile."

Yes, good . . . type: **Thanks . . .** and

Hit Send.

Quickly I turn off the computer. I feel wired, like I just went through the whole battle with Irgan again.

This is why I never e-mail people between rounds. It's like, Be who you are in the Game, I don't need to know you.

And I don't want anyone knowing me.

FOUR

Most people have good days or bad days. My mom has okay days and wretched days. At least, that's how it seems since she started her new job. At first she was psyched, because it pays pretty well. Basically she tells people what to do with their money. But I guess anything that pays well makes you work really hard and drives you crazy. Because ever since she started, there've been a lot of nights when she comes home and says, "What a wretched day."

Like tonight. She came in, handed me the phone, and said, "Sushi deluxe for me, whatever you want for you." And all through dinner she's done nothing but complain. While I nod my head and act like I understand it all.

Finally, though, she gets bored with it and snaps on a big smile. "So! Talk to anyone at school today?"

And I'd rather she went back to complaining again, because I know she means Leia.

Well, Mom, she totally burned me in the lunchroom. But it's okay. I burned her back.

Nope, not what Mom wants to hear.

I smile. "Crazed day."

She echoes my smile. "Talk to *anybody?*"

Uh, a witch—but a good one, Mom, you'd like her. A warrior who's drunk most of the time. Oh, and a murderous psychopath.

I shake my head. "Just too crazed."

It is a small problem. When your whole life is something you can't talk about.

After dinner I'm on my way back to my room, when my mom says, "Hey . . . ," and points to the garbage. Like, *I don't care what fantasy world you're in, young lady, the garbage still goes out.*

Which, yes, Mom, I know.

In our building you have to take the garbage down to the basement. So I go out to the hall to wait for the elevator.

Behind the Heitmans' door I hear the TV. Low voices, then a burst of gunfire. Sounds like a cop show. The reality one where the cops always end up flinging the guy onto the ground and putting on the cuffs.

Maybe Jonathan's studying up for his future as a criminal.

In the elevator I watch as the light descends along the floor numbers. Twelve . . . eleven . . . nine . . . six . . . three . . . lobby.

The elevator stops at the lobby. But whoever pressed for it must have given up, because there's nobody there.

I hit B again, even though I already pressed it, and the door slides shut.

There's a grinding, rattling sound, like the cables are just letting go, dropping you down, down. . . .

Confession: I hate the basement.

For one thing, it's dark. The wiring is so old it can't support more than a few weak lights. The ceiling's really low, and the floor is all uneven. And it smells. Dank. Like a cave.

The basement didn't used to creep me out. But a few months ago a woman got mugged in our building. Mrs. Buck, who lives in 6E. There are different stories about where she got mugged. Some people say it was in the lobby when she went to get her mail.

And some people say she was down in the basement doing laundry.

Or that whoever did it got in through the basement.

I call out, "Hello."

No one answers. I can hear the boiler rumbling in the back.

Taking a deep breath, I start heading down the long

corridor that leads to the garbage room. There are doors on both sides of the corridor; they look like prison cells. Like something weird and violent is going on behind them. I bet they haven't been opened for years.

Basement: The Game. Descend to the deepest realm of evil and . . .

Face GIANT RATS! Escape EXPLODING BOILERS! Fend off PSYCHOPATHIC CREEPS!

I think that's a game I'll be avoiding.

At the end of the hall, on the left, there's the laundry room. On the right is the room where they keep the garbage bins.

I'm just going to open the door and chuck the stupid garbage bag in. It's tied up tight, it won't open.

I push, feel the door give under my fingers.

And from inside I hear something move. . . .

People do come in here. They don't keep the courtyard door locked properly. Freaks and addicts come in here, and they are not in their right mind. . . .

I am not breathing. And because I'm not breathing, I can't run.

And because I can't run, I am dead.

Whatever it is, is coming toward the door. I step back as the door swings open.

Jonathan Heitman.

For a second we just stare.

I hear myself breathing. Embarrassed, I stop, hold my breath.

Because I don't know what else to do, I step inside, toss the bag into one of the bins.

I say, "Sorry." And hate myself.

Jonathan doesn't say anything. Instead he reaches out . . .

You have discovered my secret lair. Now I shall have to kill you.

And shuts the door.

For a moment we just stand there. Two people in a stupidly small space who don't know what to do with each other.

In a low voice he says, "Anyone out there?"

"Like who?"

"Like the janitor?" He looks at me like, *How dim are you?* I shake my head.

He nods, like he's satisfied, and sits up on one of the garbage bins. He starts looking for something on the lid.

I tell myself I am not afraid of Jonathan Heitman.

But I am. A little. Everybody is.

He used to be this hyper, screaming kid with skinny arms. When we were little, he would shriek, "Jude the Prude, Jude the Prude," whenever he saw me, until his mom yanked him by the arm and told him to cut it out.

Now he's this . . . guy. And not just 'cause he's taller than me, but because of the way he moves. Like he's aware of himself. Aware of what he can do. Which makes you aware of him. Your nerves are on alert because no matter how far away he is, he feels a little too close for safety.

But he's not like football-player big. And when he pushes his hair back, I see his ears are little, pointed. He's got a strong nose, a hard mouth. But then these elf ears.

He seems way older than anybody I know at school.

He says, "Since the mugging the janitor 'patrols' the basement at night, makes sure there are no evildoers lurking." Jonathan Heitman has a rough, hoarse voice, like he smokes too much. Or just spent forty-eight hours screaming in a padded cell.

He finds what he's looking for. A joint. It figures.

You jerk, I want to tell him. *Your mom's out there working her butt off to keep you in some halfway decent school, and you're down here being a jerk.*

"How long do I have to wait?" I ask.

"Not long. He usually comes around now. If he sees you going out, he might look in here, and I don't need that."

I do not want Mr. Dalmas finding me in here with Jonathan Heitman and pot. "What if he checks in here anyway?"

"Dalmas? Forget it. He might have to *do* something." Jonathan coughs. "Guy's a drunk."

Yeah, I think. You should hear what he says about you.

As if he knows what I'm thinking, he takes a drag of the joint, then holds it out to me. "Care for some?"

"No." I hate the smell. Sweet. Foolish. Weak.

He smirks, like he knew I wouldn't, and goes back to it.

For some reason it's when he's not looking at me that I feel antsy. It gives me the choice to act, but I can't quite make the choice. I mean, I could just go for the door. . . .

Odds that he'd let me go if I threatened to yell: unknown.

Odds that he could grab me before I got to the door: unknown.

That's the problem. Jonathan Heitman is an unknown entity. Which makes me an unknown entity. I'm not sure what I can do, what I can't. . . .

"What's the shirt?"

I jump. I've been thinking so hard I almost forgot he was there. "What?"

He nods at me. "The shirt. The thing on your sleeve."

I look down and see what he's talking about. A while ago I went through this thing where I couldn't sleep. Insomnia is totally boring. You run out of things to do. So one night I decided to kill time by drawing the Game's symbol on the sleeves of my T-shirts.

It's really faded out now, so I'm surprised Jonathan could even see it.

"Just something I do." I've never talked about the Game to anyone. I'm not sure even how to talk about it.

"Something you do."

That feeling. Like he's going to do something, just waiting for the right moment.

Don't talk a lot. Otherwise he'll know he's making you nervous.

However many words he uses, however many syllables, I will use fewer.

"Online." Two to his four. I feel the impulse to explain, "It's a game." But that's too much.

"Something you do online. Well."

That "Well" pisses me off. It says, *Sex*. He's thinking the Game is about sex, because isn't everything online about sex?

Well, if it's not about sex, it's just sad. That's what he's thinking, I know it.

Yeah, I think, as opposed to coming down here and getting wasted, which is truly a worthwhile thing to do.

"What is it, like a chat room?"

Seven syllables . . .

"No, it's like a game." Five to his seven.

"Meet a lot of horny old guys?"

"No."

He nods like he's taking this very seriously. "Just a lot of sad, pathetic ones."

"Yeah, well, they're everywhere."

A pause. Whatever game we're playing, I just scored.

His mouth curls up. "Freak and geek time."

"Yeah, whatever."

Four to four. Stalemate. Time to go.

I reach for the door. Then I hear footsteps.

Jonathan freezes. Then slowly he raises his hand: *Just hold on*.

Without thinking, I nod.

Footsteps are closer. I hear humming. Dalmas. It's definitely Mr. Dalmas.

Nobody on this side of the door is breathing.

I listen as Dalmas trundles down the hall. At every door he knocks, calls, "Hello." His voice is happy, silly. He knows—or thinks he knows—that no one's down here.

I glance over at Jonathan. He's tense, watching the door.

"Hello, hello." Dalmas is maybe two doors away. He giggles, knocks again.

That's when I realize: Mr. Dalmas is drunk. Jonathan was right about that.

The humming's close, at the next door. I hear keys jangling.

I can't look at Jonathan. All I can do is stare at the door, wait for it to move, to open. . . .

Uh, hello, Mr. Dalmas. . . .

I'm so convinced the next thing I'm going to see is Mr. Dalmas that when I hear him call out, "Laundry room, hello," it takes me a second to realize . . .

He's on the other side of the hall. He's not coming in.

The next thing we hear is footsteps again. But fading this time as he goes back down the hall. Then the rattle of the elevator cables in the distance, and we know: It's safe.

I hear Jonathan behind me, something like a sigh. "Okay, he's gone."

I turn around. I didn't realize we were standing so close. I step back, reach for the door handle.

Then I stop. It's like when Dalmas went, something went with him that was okay, but I can't figure out what it is. I look at Jonathan, try to see if he knows.

He says, "It's cool, you can go." He's got this little smile on his face like, *God, you're sad.*

I open the door.

"Hey?"

I turn around.

"What's it called?"

I look back.

"What?"

"The . . . thing." He flips a finger toward my shirt. "The thing you do sometimes."

I tell him.

He shakes his head. "Freaks and geeks," and goes back to the joint.

In the elevator I press the wrong floor. Ten. I press ten. Instead of twelve. My hand's not working right.

I move into the corner, take a deep breath.

I can't believe I stayed there. Can't *believe* I told him about the Game.

I should have just split. The second I saw him.

When I get back, my mom is soaking in the bathtub. She hears me, calls through the door, "Hey . . ."

To cover for being so long, I call back, "I ran into Ms. Ochs in the elevator." Ms. Ochs is a real talker. She can hold you up for hours.

My mom groans in sympathy. "Ugh. You going to bed?"

"Yeah. I'm worn out."

Which is true. But when I get to my room and shut the door, I'm way too wired to sleep. I feel like I need to do something. Be anywhere but here. Be anyone but that stupid girl who got trapped in the basement with Jonathan Heitman.

Gee, Jonathan, can I go now?

No, you must stay here. I command it.

Oh, okay.

I mean, what is wrong with me?

I sit down at the computer, log on. For a while I just surf. I don't even know what I'm looking at. Search, open, search, open. Just a lot of dark and light, but it makes me feel better.

Before I shut down, I check my e-mail—even though, frankly, I've had enough human contact for the day.

One message. It came five minutes ago. No subject. Just blank.

But the Sender line is **Irgan@connect.com**.

I click twice. Read: **Fair warning, Thief. I want my shield back.**

I think, Oh, yeah? Because I don't know what it is, but Irgan seriously pisses me off.

I hit Reply. Type: **Too damn bad.**

FIVE

The next morning I wake up and think, Am I insane?

I must be insane. Who else but an insane person would challenge Irgan the Head Case?

Still. I don't see what else I could have done. I'm not giving the shield back. That would be like, *Here, kill me some more.*

But it's weird. "Too damn bad." I don't know where those words came from. They're not like me at all.

Then again, it's not me that's speaking.

It's Terryn.

The next day Figuroa9 makes peace between me and Irgan. But he lets me keep the shield as spoils of war.

Which means it should be over—but it's not.

Irgan wants his shield back. So it's just a matter of time before he comes after me again.

Now I have to watch his every move, sift it for danger, try and sense the threat level. So far he's playing it cool. He's waiting for the right time, when it can look like an accident. Or even justified.

The other players sense it too. Whenever Irgan or I move, there's a tension. *What's going to happen next? What should happen next?* Our fight has become this whole weird subplot to the story.

Some players, I bet, are rooting for Irgan. Like Fester and J-Boy. Ola probably roots for me. It's all about what you believe.

If you believe that the strong destroy the weak because they can, then you want Irgan to win. Some people think that's how the world works, so only his victory makes sense.

But I don't think that kind of world will ever make sense, and that's why I want to win.

Also I want to keep playing.

And I do. A few weeks go by and nothing happens. Our group keeps going in the quest to find the exiled ruler of Hazird. Irgan steers totally clear of me. I steer totally clear of him.

But then the group splits up.

One afternoon Figuroa9 sends Ola, Irgan, Fester, and

J-Boy on to scout ahead. Terryn is left behind to guard the camp. Fine. No problem.

Then Irgan says, **Leaving one man to watch for the enemy is foolish. I'm staying behind as well.**

You can feel it, through the air, the excitement. The *Ah, at last.*

Even I feel it, and I'm the one about to be toast.

Now the rest of the players have a choice. Do they argue with Irgan or not?

I write: **There's safety in numbers, but not when one of your numbers is Irgan. I'll be a sad, pathetic force of one, thank you.**

Then a message pops up. It's from Figuroa9.

Put it to a vote. Irgan and Terryn have spoken. Ola?

Against.—Ola

One for, two against. Fester?—Figuroa9

Long pause from Fester. Too long. I'm not surprised to read: **Who leaves a thief to guard his property? For.**—Fester

A tie. J-Boy. Your vote, please.—Figuroa9

I have never done anything to J-Boy. Nothing that would make him leave me in the clutches of the Head Case.

J-Boy?—Figuroa9

This has been going on too long. Let them settle it and let the Game move on. For.—J-Boy

Then, let it be settled at the next game.—Figuroa9

And that's it.

The next game.

Probably my last one.

Okay. So, how do you beat back a psycho killer? That's what I have eight hours to figure out.

Irgan outmaneuvered me. I have to admit that. Now there will be no witnesses. Officially Ola, Fester, and J-Boy are offscreen, in their own story, so they can't ever know what really happened. Sure, they'll find my mangled, bloody corpse when they return to camp. . . .

But they'll have to accept Irgan's story of how it got that way.

Luckily, after math I have a free period, so I head downstairs to the library. I'm thinking so hard I don't see anyone around me. All the way down the hall, I guess other people are there, but I wouldn't know it.

And that's how I make the mistake.

That's how I run into Leia Taplow.

As I'm heading to the library she's coming the other way. Of course she's not by herself, she's with her new friends.

They see me first and slow down. I can tell they're going into the library too. There are too many of them; I can't get by, be invisible.

So, for a second or two, we all have to be there in the hall together.

Me and . . . Leia Taplow.

And Jessica. And Kelsey.

Yeah, hi, everybody.

Leia would like to go into the library. But to do that she has to get through me. Which means she has to acknowledge I'm here. Something she hasn't done since last year.

Jessica and Kelsey frown, move in closer to Leia. Like they think it's their job to protect her from me.

It's like, *Hi, she dumped me, okay? I won't bite.*

But Leia's very good at that. Making you feel like you have to take care of her. For a second I remember how we used to go to scary movies, and she'd curl up in her seat and hide her eyes, whispering, "Oh, my God, tell me when it's over. Can I look now? Is it okay?" And I'd laugh and say, "No, definitely not yet. No . . . wait . . . okay, now. Now you can look."

Here's what I'd like to do. I'd like to look Leia Taplow right in the eye and wait.

Wait for her to say something.

Wait for her to get it that I didn't do anything to her.

But I can't look Leia Taplow in the eye. If I do, I feel like I'll see how she sees me. Everything she's decided about me. And I can't take that. I'm not strong enough yet not to care.

"Excuse me." Finally it's Leia who speaks. She pushes by me to open the door. Her bag swings into me as she goes by.

But only because I refuse to move. And I do. I refuse.

Let her get by me. I don't care. But I'm not moving to suit her.

Once Leia's through, her friends follow behind, practically running into the library.

And inside they'll wait. And before they leave, they'll check to make sure I'm gone. Make sure it's safe to come out.

What atoms do is bond. They chase one another around and hook up with other atoms. They keep hooking up until they form a whole unit, a complete compound. Some atoms need to hook up with a lot of other atoms to be complete. Some need only one.

But in a bomb atoms definitely do not bond. They collide.

I don't go into the library. Let it be Leia's domain. I have other problems to worry about.

In my head I run through all the possible scenarios for today's game. Irgan attacks, Irgan doesn't attack. I imagine lots of different rolls of the die. Lots of different outcomes.

In my ideal world this is how it goes.

Irgan raises his sword. . . .

Terryn dives. . . .

Sword is impaled in the wall. Irgan is helpless for a split second. . . .

Terryn puts a knife to Irgan's throat, says, "Now we make peace."

Or something like that.

■□■□

But I don't get my ideal world.

Irgan attacks. He attacks right away.

Two moves into the game, and his sword is at my throat.

I have one roll. If I get a six, I'm out from underneath his sword.

Anything less than a six, and I'm dead.

What can match aggression?

Nothing. Not this time. Only luck.

And I don't feel lucky.

I look at the screen. If Figuroa9 wanted to stop this, he would have done it by now.

But nothing. He's silent.

I put my hand on the mouse. Take a deep breath.

Six. I need a six. Anything less is not acceptable.

Six. I think it hard. Try and brand it on my brain.

Sixsixsixsixsixsixsixsixsixsixsixsixsix.

All it is, is a little pressure. . . .

Who cares? I think fiercely. Who cares? If they let you be attacked, if they leave you unprotected, who cares about this game?

The thoughts keep pounding in my head. And when I'm feeling my most angry, I click.

Roll of the die . . .

It's not a six.

It's the farthest from six you can get.

It's a one.

The Game has definitely spoken.

Good, I think. I'm glad to be dead. Glad to be out of it . . .

But I'm not.

Dead, that is.

Next message.

Irgan lowers his sword. Steps back.

At first I don't get it. I still think it's coming, the message "Terryn dies."

Then I do get it. But I can't believe it.

Irgan, you have won. It is your right to kill your opponent.—Figuroa9

I feel rage. Rage at being thrown over, of having Irgan chosen over me. Of all the times Figuroa9 could have spoken up, he chooses now?

From Irgan: **It's also my right not to.**

Furious, I type: **Go ahead. By all means.**

Nothing from Irgan. No kill move, no statement. Zilch.

Figuroa9: **Irgan, you have to play the Game seriously. You started a fight, now you must acknowledge and enforce the consequences.**

For what seems like forever I wait. We all wait.

Then from Irgan: **No.**

I half smile. I cannot believe this.

Reason?—Figuroa9

No reason. It amuses me.—Irgan

Then: **I like Terryn as an opponent. He amuses me too.**

But Terryn lost. Terryn must suffer the consequences.—Figuroa9

We wait, but there's no immediate answer. I feel like a maiden tied to a tree, and two dragons are fighting over who gets to fry me.

Actually, dummy, Irgan's trying to save you. The mad slasher just turned white knight.

Figuroa9's thinking the same thing, because he writes: **Irgan, mercy is not in your nature. It's a betrayal of your character.**

This is a serious sin in the gaming world. You don't betray your character. You are who you are.

I decide who I am. I decide what's a betrayal and what's not.—Irgan

For a long time no one says anything. Then Figuroa9 says: **Someone has to suffer the consequences.**

Okay, this is crazy. This has nothing to do with what's right or wrong; this is Figuroa9 acting like a badass because he's been challenged for control.

I type: **This should be up to all the players. Not the game master.**

Oh? Those same players who left you in the tender care of the Head Case?—Figuroa9

I don't know what to say to that. The fact is, something got screwed up in this game a long time ago.

Figuroa9 writes: **One of you must leave the Game.**

One of us. Me. It should be me.

God, this sucks.

Then Irgan writes: **Fine. I'm out.**

No. This is not ending like this.

Wildly, I type: **This is insane. This is not fair.**

Figuroa9 shoots back: **Fair? Who said the Game was fair? The Game's about life. Word to the clueless—that's not fair either.**

I stare at the screen. It takes me maybe two seconds to make up my mind.

You're right. Life's not fair. But the Game should be. I'm out.—Terryn

That night I can't sleep. No matter what I do, lie on my side, lie on my back, whatever. My brain will not stop buzzing.

I get out of bed and open the window. I sit on the sill and look down at the city. I keep one foot inside, put the other on the ledge. Twelve floors up.

From my window you can see everything. The world. Maybe not really, but that's what it feels like. There's so much sky. So many buildings. The streets so far below you they're like rivers.

Thousands of windows. A million lights. Life going on everywhere.

A lot of people leave their lights on. It's strange. You can see everything. I wonder if they mind that. If they know. If they even like it. The idea that someone is watching.

When you're watching someone, it's like you're the only people in the world. No matter how far apart you are.

I look down, see a woman walking her dog. She has no clue I see her, that I even exist.

How long would it take me to reach the ground from here?

Five seconds? Three? I bet it'd be the longest five seconds of my life.

I remember that old story, that if you dream you're falling and you hit the ground in your dream, you're dead.

I had that dream once. I decided to hit the ground.

Woke up anyway.

I don't get it. Why did Irgan not kill me?

For weeks that's all he played for. And then when he got the chance, he just let it go.

Why?

My eyes travel over the hundreds and hundreds of windows. Maybe Irgan's in one of them.

Or maybe he's in a house in Altoona, PA.

Or an apartment in Quebec.

Or prison.

Is it weird if I miss him?

SIX

Someone said the first atomic bomb looked like a garbage can with fins on it. It was ten feet long and weighed almost ten thousand pounds. They called it Little Boy. The next bomb, the one they dropped on Nagasaki, was called Fat Man. It weighed almost eleven thousand pounds.

I've seen the plane they carried it in. It's in a museum in Washington. It's a big plane, a B-29. My dad says it's the one they used for heavy lifting.

My dad says the whole point of modern weapons is you don't have to see the people you kill. That they're a million miles away and all you do is press a button.

Which is a weird thought. That someone so far away from you could be so dangerous.

But what freaks me out is that the bombs aren't so big anymore. Now they come in suitcases. Briefcases. You walk by someone on the street, and you see them with a backpack, and you think, Okay, the world could end right now.

Never agree to meet anyone in person.

My mom has said it a hundred times.

And I always said I wouldn't.

I couldn't understand why she was so bugged about it. Like, how stupid does she think I am?

So why am I thinking about it?

Not that I'm going to do it.

But I am going to e-mail Irgan. And I'm not sure what happens after that.

If he asked, would I meet him?

Of course not. But e-mail's not meeting. You are where you are, he is where he is.

Still. Just to see his address typed in—**Irgan@ connect.com**—feels weird. It brings him too close.

Then why send him an e-mail, I think, if you don't want him near you?

Because . . .

Because he wasn't who I thought he was, and now I want to know who he is.

You sure about that?

No. But I'm going to do it anyway.

What to write first? "Dear Irgan" is definitely out.

Finally I type: **Question.**

Okay. And the question is . . . what?

I start with: **Why did you let me go?**

No. Sucks. Delete.

Maybe simple is no good. Maybe I should be detailed, precise. But formal, not friendly. Not . . . asking for friendship.

> **I don't understand. Please explain why**
> **1. You singled me out for attack**
> **2. When you won the battle, you didn't kill me, as was your right**

I hesitate for a second, then keep going.

> **Why did you leave the Game? Were you sick of it? Did you attack me, hoping you'd get thrown out? If you hate the Game, why did you play at all?**

> **Why did you try to make everyone hate you? Do you want people to hate you?**

I type this without thinking, fingers running all over the keyboard. Then I stop.

I can't ask all this. He'll think I'm insane.

Never agree to meet anyone in person.

At some point I'm going to tell my mother you don't always agree to meet people. Sometimes people just happen to you.

Anyway.

Question.

It's like rolling the die. Don't think, just do.

Why am I still alive?

Hit Send.

I'm too scared to look at my e-mail for the rest of the evening. I keep imagining Irgan writing back, "What kind of pathetic sow are you? Get a life."

Or something worse. Much worse.

> *Dear Ms. Ellis,*
> *We at the Blatt Institute for the Criminally Insane kindly request that you cease and desist all communication with our patients.*

I mean, after all my mom's yelling it would be some kind of sick justice that I actually hook up with a serial killer.

That night, when my mom's asleep and the whole apartment is quiet, I get out of bed and turn on the computer. In the dark the screen is super bright; when it snaps on, it flashes, hurts my eyes.

If he has written back, I'll have to be careful about opening the message. It could have some weird virus, melt my whole system. That's definitely the kind of thing Irgan would do.

I open e-mail. No new messages.

Something inside me goes dead when I see that. I was so sure he would answer.

Possibility: Irgan lives in the Ukraine. There's about eight hours' difference between us and the Ukraine. So maybe he just hasn't read the message yet.

Probability: really, really low.

Two days later and still no message. Wherever he lives, he would have read his e-mail by now. Even in Outer Mongolia.

I don't get that. I don't get how you go through something so intense and then have no interest in talking to the person who went through it with you.

I have to find out who he is. It's probably totally impossible, but I feel like I have to try.

In the Game nobody uses their real name, that's a given. So, if I am Irgan, what is my actual name?

I get out my notebook. At the top of a fresh page I write, "IRGAN."

Nagir. Rinag. Aring. Ginar.

Well, hello, Mr. Ginar, how are you today?

Somehow, I don't think so.

I go back to my computer, look up *Irgan* online.

It's a Spanish word for something. It's the last name of a professor at the University of Istanbul. And it's a restaurant in San Diego.

So, okay. The person I'm looking for is a Spanish professor who teaches in Turkey and lives in San Diego.

Or . . . not.

The phone rings, and for a second I freeze. Because you can get phone numbers off the Web. You can find out where people live. Then my mom knocks at the door.

Honey, someone named Irgan? Says he wants to eat your eyeballs?

She opens the door. "Your dad's on the phone."

My mom never says anything bad about my dad. For her it's kind of like he doesn't exist. Whenever he calls, she says maybe three words to him, then hands the phone to me. And then I always feel like I have to be extra nice and talk a lot. Sort of show him, *Hi, we don't all hate you here.*

"Hey, Dad."

"Hey, kiddo. How are you?"

"Good," I say.

We do: "How are you? I'm good too. That's good." Then my dad says, "So, what's up?"

"Uh, not much. School, work, you know."

"How's your game going?" he asks, because I once told him about it.

"I'm not so into it anymore."

"No?"

"Nah. I was playing with this group, and they almost let me get killed."

"That's not very nice."

"That's how I felt, so I said . . . *sayonara.*"

"I can understand that."

Then we both wait.

Sometimes I feel like telling my dad, *You don't actually have to do this. We could wait until I graduate or get married. 'Cause maybe then we'll have something to talk about.*

I'm not mad at him for leaving, going to Seattle. Frankly, there were a lot of times when he and my mom were together when I wanted to leave. When he told me he was going, all I could think of was, I'm envious. He gets to escape.

But here's what I am mad at. That they get to not deal with each other, but I still have to deal with everybody. Like they don't care anymore, but I'm still this link between them. My dad always asks, "How's your mom?" and I want to say, "What would you do if I said, 'Terrible'?"

It's like, if you want to be here, then be here. If you want to be somewhere else, be there. But this in-between crap is ridiculous. The world is cubes. And I don't care what cube you pick. But pick one. And stay there.

But I know that's unfair. My dad's trying to do the right thing. Only it's one of those situations where there kind of isn't a right thing. Just sucky and less-sucky things.

I've broken *Irgan* down into numbers. *I* is the ninth letter of the alphabet, and so on.

    I=9
    R=18
    G=7

A=1
N=14

I don't think Irgan thinks this way. Not from the way he plays the Game. But numbers usually tell me something.

I'm sitting in the hallway, waiting to go into English. In the margin of my notebook I multiply nine by one, which makes it nine. Nine is half of eighteen. Seven is half of fourteen. A name made up of halves.

Which means . . .

Irgan is half a person.

Which makes no sense.

Or. Or not halves. Doubles. Like he's . . . schizo. Not one half, but two halves. Two different people. A person and a persona.

The door bursts open and people start pouring into the hallway, gasping and choking like they need oxygen. It's Ms. Isaacs's "Math for Dummies" class.

I think Leia's in that class.

I look. Hate myself for looking.

The thing is, I think if I could just talk to Leia alone, away from K&J, she might possibly be a human being.

But I don't see Leia. As the crowd thins out and the last kids leave I see Katie Mitchell, held up at the door by Ms. Isaacs.

Katie's saying, "Seriously, my brain does not work like this. It so does not compute this stuff."

Trust Katie Mitchell to screw up even in "Math for

Dummies," the official pass/fail playground for kids who deem it beneath them to think. *Daddy said I didn't have to.*

Ms. Isaacs says gently, "I'd be happy to work with you after school if you feel that would help. Or if you'd prefer a different tutor . . ."

Katie starts explaining how she drove her last tutor to drugs. Very quietly I get to my feet and join the crowd going into English.

You could walk a different route, I tell myself as I get near 158 West Seventy-first Street. No rule in the universe says you have to walk down this block.

Walk up just one little block. Then 158 West Seventy-first Street would cease to exist.

But the thing is, it wouldn't. It would still be there. Places and things with bad energy are like dogs. They can tell when you're afraid, and it makes them bolder, more aggressive.

Then I think: Get real, it's a door. It has no freaking clue whether you walk past it or not. Just turn right now and get it over with.

But I can't. I'm frozen. Whatever I tell myself, it just feels wrong. Out of sync. Twenty down, three across; that's how it works. Maybe it's ridiculous, but I feel like if I change direction, I'll get completely lost.

Finally the light in front of me changes: Go.

And I do.

But my brain is wide open this time. I try. I try hard to

shut it down, but the closer I get, the more it screams. I can feel the door ripple as I pass. Energy pouring off it, getting close to me, like heat.

When I make it to the next corner, I just stand for a long time, watching the light change from stop to go, stop to go.

I really miss the Game. All I want to do is go home and switch my head over to it completely.

And I could. If Irgan hadn't attacked me.

If I hadn't lost.

If, if, if . . .

God, screw Irgan—whoever he is.

But weirdly, thinking about him, I feel calmer. Like my mind has somewhere to go.

Irgan . . . Grain . . . Angir . . .

Anger?

As I wait for the elevator I wonder if maybe I should just leave it alone.

I mean, maybe Irgan's married with a million children. Maybe he really is a psychopath.

The elevator bounces to a stop. The door slides open and I step in. This thing is so old and rickety it's amazing it's never crashed. People complain all the time, but the building never does anything.

I press twelve. As I do I see Jonathan's stupid swastika, still there on button six. How long does it take to replace a button?

They're old, though. Black with a thick copper plate around them. They probably don't make this kind of thing anymore. It's really nice. The copper's all knobbly, and there's a little plaque at the bottom with the name of the company that made the elevator, probably a hundred years ago.

I look to see the name. That's when I see it.

IRGAN & CO.

THE BEST IN CONSTRUCTION SINCE 1926.

SEVEN

I can't believe it. I can't believe I am this stupid.
    Every single day I get into this elevator. . . .
    And I never saw it.
    I mean, there it is, carved into the brass:

    IRGAN & CO.
    THE BEST IN CONSTRUCTION SINCE 1926.

    Which means . . .
    I can't decide if it does mean that or not.
    "What's it called?"
    "What?"

"The thing you do sometimes."

Think. Think. Other people in the building who could be into the Game. Names and faces fly through my head. Every one of them just makes me laugh. Like Mrs. Levine from 1C playing the Game. Right.

Nobody fits.

Except Jonathan.

I mean, there are other kids in the building. But they're all little.

It can't be Jonathan.

Except it has to be.

And the other question is, How long has he known that it's me?

The second I get into my house, I go straight to my room, straight to my bureau, and start rummaging through the drawers.

But I can't find it. The shirt I was wearing that night.

Where could it be?

The hamper . . .

We keep the dirty-clothes hamper in a closet near my mom's bathroom. I go into the closet, pull the chain to turn on the light, and start picking through the old dirty clothes.

It's way down at the bottom. Of course.

I pull it out, and it's all crumpled. I shake it out and look at the sleeve. The sign of the Game is there. But what else? There has to be something else. Something that gave me away . . .

I put my palm in the sleeve, hold it flat.

And there it is. Worked into the Game symbol.

A little *T.* For *Terryn*.

So now I know who Irgan is.

Next question—Who is Jonathan Heitman?

At dinner that night I say, "Ma?"

"Ye-es?" She thinks she's imitating me.

"You know how Jonathan got kicked out of school last year?"

"Um-hm." She narrows her eyes, a sign that this is not her favorite topic of conversation.

"Do you know why?"

She sighs. "Not really. Why? Do you know?"

"No. What do you mean, 'Not really'?"

"I know what everyone's saying, but I don't know what actually happened. So I can't say I know because it's all just gossip. Although in Jonathan's case . . ."

"What?"

"Well, he's always been a pretty troubled kid."

So you believe everything bad about him, I think, and that's totally unfair.

But is it? A person is what he does, and Jonathan has done a lot of rotten things. Things he doesn't even think are rotten. Which somehow makes it worse.

I ask, "So, what're the rumors?"

"Oh, I bet you can guess."

"Come on. Tell me."

"Well, uh . . ." My mom sighs. "Like drugs. For one thing. People say that he got caught with them at school, and that's why the school expelled him."

"That's weird, why bring them to school?"

My mom smiles a little. "Well, to sell them, hon."

"Oh." Yeah, I guess they would kick you out for that. "What kind of drugs?"

"I don't know. Why?"

"Well, were they, like, serious or, like . . ." My mom is staring at me, and I think, Oops, big mistake. Do not say some drugs are serious and some are not. "I mean, I know he smokes pot."

"How do you know?" My mom is all intense now. *Where were you on the night of the twelfth?*

"Because I've seen him around the building." My mom is still watching me, so I roll my eyes. "Oh, yeah, Mom, I am his biggest customer."

"Don't be. Not even his smallest, tiniest customer . . ."

"Yes. I know."

"I mean it, not any, not at all. Do you hear me?"

"Um, yes, you are right across the table from me." My mom looks fierce, and for a second I feel bad for being snotty to her. Still, I wish she wouldn't always freak out.

"So," I say, "not even a subatomic customer."

"Nope."

"Not even molecular, particular . . ."

"Not even."

But she's grinning now. Her math-geek daughter is back.

"Not even a corpuscle or a millimeter or a fraction."

And my mom starts laughing, all the while saying, "Nope, nope. No to that one. Nope."

Later, as we wash the dishes, she says, "Seriously, hon. I don't like to say this, but Jonathan's always been a very angry kid. And maybe he has some reason to be, but I'd stay away from him."

When the dishes are done, I start tying up the garbage. My mom says, "I don't think it needs to go yet."

I smile. "If you don't, it gets stinky."

As I wait for the elevator I think: You have no clue that he's down there. You have no clue it's even really him.

Except it is. I know it is.

The elevator comes. I get in. Press B for basement.

And start heading down.

As I walk toward the garbage room I wonder if Jonathan can hear me. If he thinks I'm the janitor. I imagine him sitting completely still, pretending he's not there.

I take the doorknob in my hand, twist, and give the door a gentle push. It starts to open. Slowly.

The door swings wide, and I see him. His eyes are intense, fixed on the door.

Funny, he had the time to put on his *Who gives a crap?* face.

But he didn't.

I say, "It's you."

"It's me."

He takes a drag. Coughs a little.

"Sorry, who's me?"

A thump of disappointment. He's not going to admit it. Game over.

But then I think, No, this is all just part of it.

"Irgan," I say. "The Game."

No sign of recognition.

"It was you, I know it."

He gives a half grin. "This is that thing you do?"

"That thing *you* do."

"You think I'm somebody in it. In the . . . Game."

I nod.

Jonathan laughs. "Uh, no—that would be the fifty-year-old horny loser who wants you to meet him in a dark corner of the park."

"And who happens to live in a building that has an elevator built by Irgan and Company?"

Jonathan's eyes narrow. But the smile doesn't slip. He's trying to do *You're nuts.* But it's not working.

"Come on. I know it's you."

He shakes his head. "It's not actually me. Sorry."

Friendly, nice. Like, *Sorry, you're pathetic, but there's nothing I can do about it.*

"Okay," I say. "If that's the way you want it."

"That's the way it is," he says.

And it's just like it was in the elevator. I know he's

lying. But I can't get what I know is true to be real.

So there's nothing I can do except say, "Fine," and disappear.

Back in my room I sit on my bed and try to do my homework. But instead I just end up drawing a dark line in the margin of my notebook. I draw it over and over, seeing how deep and dark I can get it before it rips the page.

I glance at the clock on my desk. Not even nine thirty.

I bet Leia hasn't even started her homework. Nine to ten she watches that dumb show about the girl and the two guys. *Will she pick the blond one or the brown-haired one? Tune in next week. . . .* You never ever call Leia between nine and ten on Tuesdays. Before or after is okay.

Used to be okay.

I wonder what she'd do? If I called her right now?

Probably get her mom to answer, like she did the last time. "I'm sorry, dear, Leia's not home." I wish I'd had the guts to say, "Give me a break."

I hate when people do that. Pretend they're not there.

"Sorry I missed your call, kiddo."

Pretend they didn't see you.

I do not acknowledge your existence. . . .

That it wasn't them, when it was.

"It's not actually me. Sorry."

I turn to the next page in my notebook. At the top of the page I write:

I am Judith Ellis, and Judith Ellis is
(smartnicegoodkinddiligenthelpfulalwaysdoes
herhomeworkpleasuretohaveinclass).
Who cares?
Who CARES?

I tear out the page and throw it away.

When the doorbell rings, I barely notice it. I mean, it's not like it's for me.

Which is why it's totally weird to hear my mother say, "Jonathan. How are you?"

Then Jonathan: "Good. Good."

I get up, open the door the tiniest crack.

"Do you need something? Are you locked out?" My mother, I can tell, has not let him in yet. I imagine her standing, smiling, in the doorway.

"Uh, no . . . I'm, uh, here to see Jude."

I can't tell which is stranger: hearing Jonathan Heitman's voice in my house or hearing him talking to my mother.

And I can't believe he's still calling me Jude. But weirdly, it doesn't bug me.

"Oh. Well. Judith?" my mom calls. But not loud. She's hoping I can't hear her, hoping I have my headphones on, so she can say, "I'm sorry, Jonathan, she's not here."

I open my door, step out into the hallway. Say, "Yeah, here."

It's true. Jonathan Heitman is almost in my house.

"It's Jonathan?" My mom gives me a look like, *Explain, please. How is this happening?*

"Hey." Jonathan waves. He knows perfectly well he's giving my mom the freaks, but it just kind of amuses him.

I guess it kind of amuses me, too, because all of a sudden I feel like laughing.

I say, "Are you here to see the thing?"

"Yeah," he says. "The thing."

"Cool. Come on."

EIGHT

Okay, right now there are two realities of varying weirdness and intensity.

One is my mother, sitting in the living room and fuming: *What is Jonathan Heitman doing in my daughter's room?*

And the other is Jonathan Heitman. Actually in my room.

But so far he hasn't said anything. All he's done is glance around my room. I watch him taking it in, try to see it through his eyes. The blue rag carpet I used to pretend was an island when I was a kid; my desk and computer, cleaned up, because that's how I like it. In fact, the messiest thing is my shelves, because I have way too many books.

He looks at my bed, and I kind of wish Katherine, my old stuffed hippo, weren't sitting on the pillow grinning back at him. Then I feel disloyal and think, Sorry, Katherine.

I never actually realized: This is not that big a room.

I can't tell what Jonathan thinks. He smiles a bit at my mushroom cloud poster—suprageek—but that's all he shows.

Then he goes over to my bed and looks out the window. People have started putting holiday lights up in their windows, and for a second it seems like he's staring at them.

Then he turns around. "You guys definitely get the better view. You can't see squat from our place."

He sits up on the sill, asks, "You know what's weird?"

Right now? Only everything. I shake my head.

"I never even thought about the elevator."

"You're kidding." I sit up on my desk.

"No. I guess it just stuck in my head, and later I thought, Oh, hey, cool name." He shakes his head. "I couldn't figure it out, how you knew."

"When did you figure it out? About me?"

He grins. "Well, the T-shirt was kind of a giveaway."

"Yeah, but did you know I was . . ." I don't know why I can't say "Terryn," why it feels embarrassing all of a sudden.

"Nah, man, I thought you had to be Ola. Then just when I'm about to pound this annoying tick named

Terryn, he comes out with something that sounds strangely familiar. . . ."

Just a lot of sad, pathetic ones.

Just a sad, pathetic force of one. . . .

"And I thought, Man, she's twisted."

I slide off the desk, sit in my chair. The chair spins and I turn to face him. "Gee, thanks. From a psycho killer, that's quite the compliment."

He folds his arms. "You annoyed me. Creeping around, doing your sneaky thief thing. 'Oh, nobody look at me, I'm not doing anything.' You needed to be drawn into honest combat."

That surprises me, that he would see Terryn like that. I just figured he thought, Hey, little guy. I can destroy him, easy.

Swaying in the chair, I say, "That wasn't honest, that was slaughter. You were a hundred times stronger than me."

Jonathan raises his hands. "Hey, I let you go. Not my fault that dipwad Figuroa9 screwed it up."

"Why did you? Let me go?"

"Because it was a great twist."

I look at him like, *Yeah, right.*

"Really. The whole thing had gotten so predictable. Good was good, evil was evil. Victim"—he points to me, then himself—"villain. Boring. Where's the challenge if you already know everything up front?"

There's something in what he's saying, but I can't tell what.

He says, "Come on, you have to admit, we made a good story."

I tap my thumb on the desk. "People were into it, yeah."

"It was the best moment when I let you go. Nobody expected that." Then he says casually, "You were a decent twist yourself. I didn't see that one coming."

Okay, a compliment from Jonathan Heitman. Talk about things you don't expect.

I pick up a pencil, let it drop back down on the desk. "You should start your own game."

"Nah." He glances out the window. "I'm kind of over the online thing."

I tell myself I did not expect Jonathan Heitman to say, "Why, yes. I am starting a game. Want to play?" But the stomach drop of disappointment tells me I'm a liar.

"I mean, don't you think those games are pretty limited?" he says.

"No." To me, the Game is the only unlimited thing in the world.

"Like, you can only do this if you get this number, or be this if you get to this certain place."

"You have to have rules. It's a game."

"Why?" He looks at me. "What about a game where there are no rules?"

I am learning: Sometimes Jonathan mentions things just to confuse you. It's a negative, a check, a block.

But this isn't one of those times. He's all energy, leaning forward, waiting for me to answer.

Match him, energy for energy, I tell myself. Say yes. Say it right now.

Instead I wimp out, say something about the computer.

He waves a hand. "Forget the computer. Forget the code, forget the whole regimented deal. Just characters. And action. People do things. Other people do things back." He grins.

"That's not a game."

"Who says?"

"You don't win."

"No. You just keep playing."

Those are magic words. A game that does not end. A game that doesn't have to start and finish.

"It's in your head," he says. "Just going all the time . . ."

"But . . ."

"Yeah?"

"Who are we?" I feel shy asking it.

"Whoever you want to be."

"Do we roll—?"

"No. No. Forget the dice. You decide who your character is. I could never stand that crap. How you couldn't even decide who you were and what you could do."

I think. "So, it's like a story. Or a movie."

"Yeah. With . . ." He thinks about it, the right word. "Twists."

Of course, his favorite. "And we act it out."

"We write it, man. It's ours."

Ours. The word reminds me I'm going to be doing this with Jonathan Heitman.

I glance at the computer. Because there are other games.

Jonathan says, "Hey, we're both out, we might as well do what we want."

I think. "We need a situation. A setting, at least."

"I can do that."

"Oh, you're appointing yourself game master?"

"You think of one, I don't mind."

What else is dangerous here? "What's your character?"

"Haven't decided yet. Depends on who you are."

"Why?"

"Because." He shrugs. "It has to be a good combination. You can't have two characters with no tension. They have to match in some way."

"And completely not match in other ways," I say.

"Yeah." He nods. "Exactly."

For a second we just look at each other. Like we can't actually believe we agree.

"So, these characters."

"Yeah?"

"What do we do with them?"

"Anything. Anything we want."

I'm on the verge of saying, "Yeah, okay," when I think of something else I have to ask.

"Why didn't you just admit it? Downstairs, when I asked?"

He smiles. "Never admit anything."

There's a knock at the door. For some reason I immediately check where I am, where Jonathan is, before calling, "Yeah?"

The door opens. My mom looks in.

"Hi." She smiles at me. Then at Jonathan, as if remembering just now that he's here. "Hi, Jonathan. Judith? Were you going to show me that paper you were working on?"

"Oh." I do not actually have a paper I am working on. My mom knows this. She also knows I won't announce that she's lying. "Well . . ."

"You know what?" Jonathan gets down from the ledge. "I gotta go. But um . . ."

He turns, looks at me.

I say, "I'll think about it."

"Yeah." He nods. "It's okay, Ms. Ellis, I know how to get out. Thanks."

For a moment my mom and I just listen to Jonathan walk down the hall. Then I hear the door open and shut. It's quiet for a few seconds.

"Well," says my mom, her eyes all wide. "What was that?"

She's smiling, and all of a sudden I realize that she wants this to be a big joke. *Jonathan Heitman coming over here? To see Judith? That's a complete mistake. That's never going to happen again.*

Then she asks, "So, what's this 'thing'?"

Thing? Oh. I realize my mom has been sitting out in the living room all this time, trying to imagine "things" Jonathan wants to see.

I have not decided yet whether I am going to do this. But I do know if I tell my mom that her two least favorite things in the world—Jonathan and the Game—are connected, the decision won't be mine to make.

So I say, "Something for school."

"For school?"

"Yeah, we're both doing revolutions in history, and I said he could look at my notes for the French Revolution."

"When did all this come up?"

"What do you mean?"

"When were you talking about school?"

I think. "Like a week ago. In the elevator."

My mom nods. I can tell she's not buying it, but there's nothing she can say.

"I guess it's good," she says slowly, "that he's trying harder in school."

Then she gets embarrassed. "By the way, I know you don't have a paper, I just . . ."

I smile. "Yeah, I figured that out, Mom."

"I wasn't sure if you wanted him here or not, you know? If you had invited him, or . . ."

I smile again. Because I don't know the answer. Did I? Do I?

Dear Jonathan . . .
Uck. No. Delete.
Jonathan . . .
Sounds too familiar.

"J"? Can I get away with that? It sounds fake cool, "Hey, J." Yeah, like that's me.

How about "Irgan"? Oh, wait a minute . . .

"Dear Irgan & Co."

I like that.

Okay, now that I like it, what do I write?

I think for a long time. Then it's obvious and I write quickly:

> **Dear Irgan & Co.,**
> **How do we begin?**

Hit Send.

An hour later I check my e-mail.

It is so strange to see it. **Irgan@connect.com.**

It's like a gift. Or a warning. It's too intense, and for a second I don't want to open it.

What am I doing? Talking to Jonathan Heitman? What psycho alternate universe is this?

I remember Jonathan saying, "Anything. Anything we want."

I guess it's ours.

I open the e-mail. It says: **Tell me who you are.**

NINE

Tell me who you are.
And then:

> **Introductions.**
> **2100, 12/05, 13th floor. 4th tower.**
> **Come as you are.**

I look at the calendar—12/05 is this Friday. Three days from now.

But that's the only thing about the message that makes sense.

I'm about to type back, "Explain." But then I stop.

Because it's a riddle. And in order to play, you have to figure it out.

Interesting.

Okay, 12/05 is a date. That's obvious. December, the twelfth month, fifth day. That's this Friday.

But 2100? What is that? A century? Maybe when Jonathan wants to set the new story?

No, it's a time. I'm sure it's a time. There's nothing else here that would be the time.

Suddenly I think of commando movies. Some guy in army fatigues, his face all painted up in camouflage, muttering into a walkie-talkie: "Rendezvous at 0700 hours."

Midnight is 2400 hours, so count back. Nine o'clock— 9:00 P.M. on December 5.

Cool. Now we know when. But where?

Thirteenth floor. There is no thirteenth floor in the Bradnor. The twelfth is the highest it goes. Unless . . .

Some twelve-story buildings actually call the first floor Ground or Lobby. So they don't have the bad luck of having thirteen floors. I try to picture the elevator. The lobby—is it Ground or one?

It's one. One through twelve. So twelve isn't the thirteenth floor.

What's above twelve?

Nothing. The roof.

Which you can get on to. I know because every year people go up to watch the July Fourth fireworks. It's great.

You can see the whole city from there. And New Jersey across the river.

And the fourth tower? I have no idea what that is. But I guess once I'm up there, it'll be obvious.

And who will Jonathan be meeting on the thirteenth floor?

That's question number two.

It's like that old game: If you could be anyone in the world, who would you be?

I always said, "Myself," because I couldn't think of anyone else real I wanted to be. I mean, who wants to be the president? My friends always said stuff like, "Rich," or some movie star.

I get out my notebook. This is my favorite part of any game. New character, new name, new life . . .

Quickly I write, "Smart." Because I can't play a dumb person. It's just not that interesting. Dumb people never know what's going on, they have to wait for other people to tell them.

But smart isn't good enough. What kind of smart? Intelligent? (Yawn.) Brilliant? (Bleah.) Clever?

Maybe.

Clever's good. It sounds like you have a good mind, but you also know how to use it to figure the world out.

I've been thinking as Terryn for so long it's weird to switch to a whole new head. Particularly when you don't even know who the head belongs to. I keep thinking in negatives. Not wimpy, not out of it, not . . .

Not me.

Although maybe I should try being a girl this time.

I mean, it's one thing to play something totally different on the computer, where nobody can see you and nobody knows who you are.

But when you're right there in front of them . . .

I think about it, playing a girl with Jonathan. Me as Witch, me as Woman Warrior, me as Bodacious Butt-Kicking Babe. *Hi-yaa, evildoers!*

Then I laugh. Because I kind of can't imagine myself in a leather catsuit and high heels.

Question: Would Irgan have attacked Terryn if Jonathan had known I was a girl?

No.

And that's a problem. Because I didn't like being attacked, but I did like being considered a worthy opponent.

Also, I still remember when I was in the garbage room with him, how I was all like, "Oh, yes, master, whatever you want."

I'd rather be somebody like Terryn. Who would tell Jonathan to go screw himself.

People always say that about boys. They're not nice like girls, they hit people, and they don't talk about things. But who wants to be nice all the time? And why do you have to talk about everything?

People say you can be whatever you want. But that's

just crap. Nobody gets to be whatever they want. There's always expectations. I guess I'd rather be the things that boys have to be than the things girls have to be.

Only, what if Jonathan thinks that's totally queer? That I'm this total wacko?

It's not like people haven't decided that before.

It's funny. Some things you remember with your gut before your head does the pictures.

My last fight with Leia is one of those things.

All I asked her to do was play the Hell's Mouth game. Just one game. And she was totally obnoxious about it.

Part of what really pissed me off was we had just spent the entire day doing what she wanted to do. Namely, hanging out at this cheesy rock-'n'-roll restaurant because supposedly celebrities show up there, and that day Kevin Weymouth was supposed to show.

I don't know who I would be in love with if I had to be, but no way would it be Kevin Weymouth. He looks like a girl. But he's totally hot, in Leia's not-so-humble opinion.

And other people's too. The restaurant was packed, all these moronic girls going, "Where's Kevin? Is that Kevin? Oh, my God, I totally think that's him. . . ."

Even Leia. It was like her brain had melted and the only thing it could process was *Weymouth . . . Kevin . . . Weymouth.*

I tried to be nice about it, not say anything. But after three hours I was like, "Can we go now? Because he obviously isn't coming, and you know what? At this point I might throw up if he did."

90

I didn't say that. I think the most I said was, "Ooh, I think it's Kevin—just kidding."

Which was maybe a little jerky.

Leia finally agreed to leave, but I could tell she was a little pissed off. Probably if I'd let her, she'd have stayed the whole day. Instead we wound up at my house.

Where I tried to get her to play the Game.

Which was a big mistake.

I can still remember her sitting on the floor in my room, saying, "I don't get this. What do you mean I have negative forty power? God, how much math do you need to know for this stuff?"

Finally she said, "I'm sorry, this is too far into Geek City for me."

So I said, "Okay, whatever."

Then Leia said, "Please do not tell me you're seriously getting into this. I mean, God . . ." She groaned. "'Ooh, I'm an elf. Ooh, look at my sword.'"

I guess she was waiting for me to laugh, but I didn't.

"I mean, it's for lamos."

"Well, then, hi, I'm a lamo. Okay?"

And that surprised her. Obviously she expected me to say, "Oh, you are so right, Leia. Who would be caught dead with such a sad, uncool thing?"

"I mean, you're right," I said, "it's not nearly as fascinating as . . . the mall. It's not as awe-inspiring as lipstick or clothes or . . ." I wanted to say "Kevin Weymouth," but I didn't have the guts.

"It's a pathetic fantasy," she said. Her teeth were tight, which is how she gets when she's serious and threatening you. Like, *Stop this now, or I won't be friends with you.*

That really pissed me off. "Oh, right. Like mooning over Kevin Weymouth and waiting for him to show up at some restaurant like he's going to *notice* you or something—that's totally real, right? That's really going to happen. I mean, the guy's probably gay."

"You're probably gay," she shot back.

Even now I don't know what to say to that. Leia was so nasty about it I instantly wanted to say, "No, I'm not."

But I couldn't, partly because she wasn't asking me, she was yelling it at me. So whatever I thought or said was irrelevant. Sort of like saying, "Don't do that," after someone punches you in the face. Which is actually what it felt like.

So I just sat there fiddling with the mouse until I heard her say, "I gotta go." Then the door slam.

Sometimes I wonder, because I didn't say anything, what she really thinks. If she thinks I was admitting something or . . .

I mean, I don't know why she couldn't talk to me once on the phone. Why she can't even look at me at school.

I don't want to think about this anymore. I pick up my notebook again.

At the top of the page I write, "Gareth."

Because I've decided: That's who I want to be.

Oh, and must remember: Say nothing to my mom about this new game.

Because if she freaked out about online bogeymen, she'd go ballistic over Jonathan Heitman.

Only, what am I going to tell her about Friday night?

At dinner I'm trying to decide if it should be a study group or a chorus rehearsal I have to go to on Friday, when my mom says, "By the way, Friday? I'll be home late. A friend asked me out to dinner."

I look up from my book. "Which friend?"

"Lauren. From the office. You've talked to her on the phone. I'll be home by ten, but I'll leave you money for takeout. Unless you want me to make something and freeze it."

"No, takeout's fine, Mom."

"I'll tell you the restaurant we're going to and—"

"Mom, it's fine. Totally."

Then I think of something and say, "You know, and it's cool if it's not Lauren. If it's . . . Waldo or somebody."

"Waldo?" My mom laughs. "How am I suddenly having dinner with someone named Waldo?"

"I'm just saying . . ." But I don't really know what I'm saying, and I go back to my book.

Then I realize: Hey, problem solved.

Only, I hope nothing horrible happens. My mom would feel guilty for the rest of her life.

That night I'm getting ready to go to bed, when I hear a *ping!* behind me. I turn and see I have a message.

It's from Jonathan.

Subject: New Game
The new game takes place in the distant
future. Hostile environment. No stupid goal.
Just shifting alliances, struggles for power.
Trust. Betrayal. War.
More 12/05.

I stare at the message. Think, We're really going to do this.

I can't believe it.

I can't wait.

To get to the roof, you have to take the stairs. There's a door in between the two apartments that takes you into the stairwell. If there's a fire or something, that's where you're supposed to go.

When I was little, I used to love hiding there. I guess because we lived in an apartment, the zigzag puzzle of up and down seemed really neat to me. My parents would go out in the hall and wait for the elevator. And behind their backs I'd slowly inch toward the stairwell door, open it, and disappear.

I mean, not that they didn't know. They'd do this whole pretend thing: "Where's Judith? Do you see her? Where'd she go? The elevator's going to be here any minute. . . ."

And I'd stand on the other side of the door listening. But I also remember looking up and down at the stairs, thinking, Where does all that go?

So now I guess I get to find out.

I open the stairwell door. At first I think it'll be locked, but it's not. It creaks horribly, like an alarm (*Door open, door open, whoop, whoop . . .*), and as fast as I can, I slip through and shut it.

The stairs feel totally separate from the rest of the Bradnor. They're dingy, the walls are painted olive green, the windows are all grimy. It's a dark, abandoned place. The only sign that anybody's been here in the last hundred years is the cigarette butts littered all over the stairs.

It feels much colder here. You know if you spoke, it would echo.

For a second I peer over the rail, down the well of twelve flights of stairs. I can't really see the lobby floor; it gets lost in all the layers of stairs and banisters. But I know it's down there.

But I'm not going down. I'm going up. Overhead is a skylight so filthy and covered with wire you can't see the sky. But I guess that's up there too. Keeping my eyes on the skylight, I start climbing.

As I walk I try to imagine I'm Gareth. I've never had to move as a character before; I've always been sitting down. How would Gareth move? I think of Jonathan, how he walks, try to imitate it.

The landing after the twelfth floor, there is no door. Just a blank wall. Like, *You can't get out now.*

I speed up, swinging around the corner of the landing, one hand on the banister as I charge up the last of the stairs. And at the top there's the entryway to the roof. A big, battered metal door with a mean-looking dead bolt on it.

The dead bolt is for keeping people out of the building. Not off the roof. Because any thief who made it up to the roof wouldn't have anywhere to go. What are they going to do? Jump?

You could get to our roof, maybe, from some of the nearby buildings. There are three others on our block. But they're at least ten feet away, and ours is the tallest one. Even if you didn't fall the whole twelve floors, it'd be a vicious landing. Especially if you were carrying a TV or something.

And that's why nobody ever comes up here. Someone like Mr. Dalmas, I mean. He knows the roof is the last place a criminal is going to go.

At least, to escape. But they could hide up here.

I guess that's why the lock is on the inside.

Which is open now, I see. Someone's opened it.

I put my hand on the door. At first I just lean, and nothing happens. The door doesn't give at all.

I push harder and the door starts to move. It's heavy and doesn't fit very well, so it scrapes and creaks and complains . . . and then it's open, and there you are, outside at night.

It's funny how outside can be so much quieter than inside.

Stepping out onto the roof feels like walking on the

moon. The roof is paved with tar, so even when it's cold, you sink and stick a little while you walk. There are hills and gulleys, big heavy blobs of tar where they've patched the roof over the years. I always think of dinosaurs when I see those. Some mastodon getting stuck, trapped, dying. Winding up in the Natural History Museum a million years later.

I haven't been up here in forever. I think the last time was a July Fourth. My dad made fried chicken and brought up an old blanket for us to sit on. "Just like the park," he said. "Only no grass and no trees. And the tar's sticky."

There's a wall that runs all along the edge of the roof. It's not very high, but I remember when we came up here that time, he had to lift me up to see over it. Now it comes up to maybe my ribs.

So . . . towers. Where are the towers?

The first thing you notice is the water tower. This huge, old wooden barrel that stands on a high platform. The barrel's enormous, like you could swim in it. Actually, you could drown.

There is a long ladder leading up to the water barrel, but there's nowhere to stand. So that can't be the tower.

Okay, so what else is a tower?

I look back at the door I came through. It's set in a kind of box, about fifteen feet high, with the skylight on top. There's a ladder so you can get to the top, I guess if you ever have to fix the skylight.

There are four of them. One on each side of the building.

And Jonathan is standing on the one closest to the river.

Waiting for me.

I go over and stand by the ladder. I sort of expect Jonathan to come to the edge, say hi or something. But he doesn't.

So I guess I have to climb.

It's only about ten rungs. But they're old. I tell myself: Jonathan just did this. If they were rotten, he wouldn't be standing where he is now.

My head clears the edge of the tower. Jonathan steps forward, the muddy night sky behind him.

He says, "Welcome to the Academy."

TEN

The Academy, I think. Okay, interesting.

I hoist myself over the top of the ladder, onto the roof of the tower. There's a little ledge, so the floor feels kind of like a foxhole.

It's seriously cold. The wind's blowing hard.

"Thank you." I hesitate for a moment. If Jonathan's offering the welcome, clearly he's someone in charge. But how powerful? A teacher? An older student? The doorman?

"Evans." He smiles, knowing this doesn't give me even a hint as to his power.

He takes a notebook out of his pocket. "May I record the name of our new recruit?"

Recruit. Not student. What's that? It's . . . military. Like the army or something. A military academy. That's good, that gives us possibilities.

I give my name. "Gareth."

Jonathan nods. Then he says, "If you are here, that means your parents are dead. Or in prison, which means they will shortly be dead. If you are here, it means you belong to the Academy. You have no other loyalties, no other ties. You are what we make of you. Do you understand?"

I nod.

"Fine. Shall we introduce ourselves?"

Then he says, "We don't have to do this in character. We can just be ourselves."

We sit down, and even though the floor is really chilly on my butt, it's better not to be standing in the wind.

I pull my notebook out of my knapsack, say, "I brought this. In case we wanted to keep a record."

"Cool." Jonathan sits down on the ledge. He folds his arms tight, stamps his feet against the cold. "Shoot."

I hesitate. It's really scary, telling someone who you are. You keep thinking they're going to laugh. And reading my own words aloud happens to be one of my least favorite things to do.

I clear my voice. Quickly I say, "Gareth is in his mid-teens. He's intelligent. Wary. Resourceful. Intuitive about people . . . and loyal."

Loyal. I'm not sure where that one came from. I was trying to think of an adjective that would deal with connection somehow, this person's sense of other people. I'm not 100 percent sure *loyal* is the right word. But you should always have a quality you're not sure about. That's usually where interesting stuff comes from.

Jonathan nods. "Okay, he's a kid. So he'll definitely be a student." He looks at me. "My guy is older, he's a teacher. Is that cool with you?"

I say, "Sure. I mean, if that's your character."

"That means I probably tell you what to do."

"Yeah . . ." I think about this. "Not all the time, though."

Jonathan considers. "Most of the time."

"Well . . ." I let a little of Gareth slip into my head. "That remains to be seen."

Then I turn the page, write down "Evans" at the top.

"Okay," I say, "you go."

Jonathan slides off the wall, crouches opposite me. For a while he stares out at the river.

Then he shakes his head. "I don't think it's a good thing for your character to know a lot about my character. It doesn't make sense."

I draw a line under the name *Evans*, start filling in the loop of the *a*. "That's a little unequal."

"They are a little unequal."

"When did that get decided?"

"One's a teacher, one's a student. Big difference in power. I mean, how would your character know anything about mine, realistically?"

101

"This isn't my character, this is the record." And I want to say, *If you think this, why didn't you say so when I was telling you all about my character? You say, "Tell me who you are," and then you pull this.*

Jonathan says, "Yeah, but if you know it, he knows it, so . . ."

"But you know everything about who I am."

"That makes sense. I would know. My character would know. It'd all be in your file."

"No." I shake my head. "No deal."

Jonathan shrugs. "Well, what then?" Like, *I'm ready to be done with this.*

I think. "You have to tell me three things about Evans. They can be true, not true. No, wait. Two can be lies. The third one has to be true. And you don't have to tell me which is which."

I look at Jonathan. He's watching me, I can feel his brain going.

He says, "How does Gareth know this stuff?"

"It's like gossip. Stuff the boys pass around about their teachers."

"Okay." He shifts his weight, holds up a finger. "Number one: He killed a student. Got in trouble for it, but it was hushed up."

"How did he do it?"

Jonathan half smiles. "All kinds of stories about that one."

"'Kay." I write it down. "And?" Jonathan frowns, grinds his sneaker into the tar. "You know, like, is he married?"

"No."

"Does he mess around with students?"

"No. Come on, don't make this into a love story."

"Okay, forget it." Message received: *Don't be such a girl.*

I wait for a second and then say, "So, what else?"

"Doesn't get along with the governor of the Academy, who's a real sleazebag operator."

"Well, that's probably true, right?"

He smiles. "You don't know. And . . ." He hoists himself back onto the ledge. "Let me think about number three, I don't have it yet."

There's a little pause. I draw angled lines in the corner of the page. Then I hear Jonathan say, "So, what's the deal?"

"Deal with what?" Even though I know what he means.

"The whole 'I only play guys' thing. I mean, Gareth's a guy, right?"

"Yeah." I run the pen over the wire binding of the notebook.

"I take it you're not into the whole chick scene."

"Not really."

He doesn't say anything. I want to get this over with now, so I say, "I mean, if you don't think I can do it or I won't be convincing . . ."

Because I am nervous about that: playing with a guy who knows I'm not one, nervous he'll tell me, "Uh, no, wrong. Guys don't do that." And I'll realize how ridiculous I've been all along.

"Ah, no, I didn't say that." He shrugs. "Frankly, it's not that amazing being one, so I was just curious."

"But it's okay."

"Sure, man, it's your character."

I watch him carefully. Because it does have to be okay. Really okay, as opposed to polite, fake okay.

But I think it is. I think Jonathan was telling the truth when he said he was just curious. I kind of like that about him, that he's curious—but he also says, "It's your thing."

Then I hear him say, "You want to start?"

Shall we begin?

"Yeah."

"As a new recruit, you will be given an assignment. A test. Are you ready?"

A test. My stomach clenches. A voice in my head. This is it, the reason you shouldn't have come, the thing you forgot about Jonathan. . . .

Part of me wants to say, "Okay, but only if it's safe. Only if we won't get into trouble."

But I can't. If Jonathan's not going to make rules with me, then I'm not going to make them with him.

Thinking Gareth, I say, "Yes."

Jonathan nods. Then he climbs down the ladder back onto the roof. I'm not sure what I'm supposed to do, but after a second I decide to follow.

By the time I get down, he's already standing by the water tower.

He puts a hand on the ladder that leans against it, closes his fingers around an old, corroded rung.

"Climb."

I stare up at the water tower, at the ladder that seems to stretch for miles. How high is it? I try to gauge. Three stories high? Four?

If I fell, would I die?

I glance over at the wall that surrounds the roof. The tower is close to the wall; probably if you fell off at a high enough point, you'd sail right over the wall, plunge twelve stories down. . . .

For a second I picture it. Arms wide, legs spread. Floating, kind of like those skydivers before their chute opens and jerks them back up.

Yeah, but you don't have a chute.

I have a weird, floaty feeling in my stomach, and my fingers are all numb. That's probably my body telling me this whole situation is bad news.

I take a deep breath to get rid of the floaty feeling. It works. For about two seconds.

I start walking toward the ladder. Think: What am I doing?

This is actually how some people die: doing dumb stuff because they don't want to look chicken.

But I'm in the game now. I said I wanted to play.

I put a hand out, touch the rung that's level with my shoulder. Jonathan must have done this himself. He has to know you can get all the way up without . . .

You have no reason to think that. No reason at all.

The ladder's really old. I bet it's rusted through in some places. The rung I'm looking at is chipped and scarred.

They've painted it over, but you can still see the worn spots, the places where the metal's really thin. Breakable.

Does anyone use this anymore? If not, wouldn't they just take it away?

But how would you get it down the stairs? Maybe they figure, Why not just leave it?

It won't hurt anybody, right?

Unless someone's stupid enough to climb it.

I can feel Jonathan is about to say something, and before he can, I put my foot on the lowest rung, reach, lift myself up.

Nothing snaps. Nothing falls.

I want to look down, see if Jonathan's surprised. But Gareth wouldn't, so I don't.

Instead I take another step up. The ladder sways. . . .

Not safe, this thing is so not safe.

Another step. I'm taller than Jonathan now. The metal is cold and scratchy under my palms. Metal gets brittle when it's cold. . . .

Another step. The ladder leans a little, bending under my weight.

What's it going to be like when I'm higher, right in the middle, the farthest point from the ground below and the landing above?

Can't think about it. Another step . . .

If this thing can hold Jonathan, it can hold me, right? I don't weigh as much as he does.

You don't know that Jonathan has ever climbed this thing.

Another step. It's almost like climbing a ladder made of ropes, the thing bends and sways so much. I take a second, breathe in . . .

Then turn my head . . .

There's New Jersey. A sea of lights. Land, safety, far, far away . . .

Above my knees I'm higher than the wall. Below it I'm still anchored. Next step and practically all of me will be past the wall.

That shouldn't matter. But it does. Somehow the wall feels like something I could grab on to if . . .

You're not going to fall. That's not going to happen.

Really? Who says?

Another step. The wind blows hard up here, blasting the hair out of my eyes. I swear, it's making the ladder move. All of a sudden I can't breathe. . . .

Hold on. Hold on. It's the only thing you can do.

Any tighter and I will break this piece of metal in my hands. I want to close my eyes, but I can't. Close my eyes and I'm lost. Look down and I'm lost. The only thing to do is look straight in front of me, not up, but straight, and keep going.

Ahead of me is other buildings. Friendly, familiar shapes. Lights are on, I can almost see people moving by their windows. You're safe. The city's around you, people are around you. You're not falling.

Another step.

All it would take, thought Gareth, is one rotten step. One crumbling, rusted rung and he would be gone. They had killed his father, would they hesitate to kill him? Or did they believe so strongly in their superiority that they felt no need to kill him? Only train him? Use him?

Was it worth it to become strong just to be used?

Thinking as Gareth, I feel calmer. Judith Ellis can die, but Gareth can't. He's the hero, and the hero can't die in the first chapter.

I lift my foot, reach for the next rung above my head. I feel the wind whipping my jeans against my legs. My hair fighting to be free of the clasp. The wall's gone now. I'm above it all. No wall, no barrier, nothing between me and sky.

The ladder's not ballooning so much anymore. I'm nearer the top. (And farther from the ground.) I have no idea, though, how far is left to go. Could be five steps, could be ten.

He could feel Evans's surprise. Not that Evans would show it, but he could feel it, Evans's eyes on him, Evans wondering, Will he really make it? Can he really pull himself all the way up?

That knowledge made the next step easy. And the next, and the next. Before he knew it, the old wooden ribs of the water barrel came into view, the harsh iron guts of the tower. For a moment he allowed himself to look beyond the rung, to take notice of where he was, how far he'd come. . . .

From the ground far below, howling above the wind, he heard, "Are you looking? What do you see?"

Clinging on, gripping the rung with his feet for all he was worth, Gareth turned his head to look out over the city, over the river, to new lands, new distances. . . .

"What do you see?"

"Everything!" I yell down.

ELEVEN

A week later I try something new. I walk home as Gareth.

I think of him heading from the student quarters to the Learning Hall. I imagine him nodding to other students, but not talking to them. I think of how he hates every single teacher there—except Evans.

When I walk past 158 West Seventy-first Street, I don't feel as freaked. It's like Gareth is a layer between that place and me, something different.

It's not like Gareth is camouflage. He doesn't make me invisible, I know that.

It's more like confusing a vicious dog with a new scent. It doesn't recognize you right away, so it forgets to attack.

From there, I start running. Away from Connolly. Away from 158 West Seventy-first Street. Away from Leia Taplow's house . . .

After five blocks I stop because I'm out of breath, walk for a while.

Then I start running again.

Until I'm home.

In the elevator, headed up to the thirteenth floor.

Today there's no assignment.

We just do the story. Evans and Gareth's meeting after the first "assignment."

"You did well," says Evans. "I confess I was surprised."

"Why?"

"We lose a lot of new recruits on that particular assignment." Evans smiles, like this amuses him. "It's an excellent tool for testing character—and dispatching the unworthy. I admit, I thought you would be dispatched."

"And now?"

"I have mixed feelings about people who surprise me. They intrigue me—but I watch them carefully. Not all surprises are pleasant ones. Perhaps," he says casually, "we should meet from time to time."

And I, as Gareth, can't tell: *Is this a good thing?*

Or a threat?

Next we do a scene with the governor of the Academy, the sleazebag who feels threatened by Evans and wonders why he's taking such an interest in a lowly new boy.

"He's nothing, a nobody, a waste of your time," I say as the governor.

"I don't think so," says Evans/Jonathan. "Meetings like this, however, are a waste of my time."

Then we decide the governor would try and play them off each other, so he calls in Gareth for a meeting too.

Now Jonathan is the governor. I move out of governor and into Gareth. What's funny is what it does to my eyes. For the governor they were narrow and suspicious; for Gareth I open them, keep them wide and blank. Show nothing.

We start. Jonathan firing questions, acting friendly, let's all be pals. But Gareth doesn't trust him, so I keep all my answers very short.

Then Jonathan says, "Break."

It takes me a second to get back into real life. "What?"

"You're acting too scared of this guy."

I stare at him. "What do you mean?"

"You're being too wimpy."

Whoa. Wait a minute. Now Jonathan is telling me what to do with my character? "I think Gareth would be a little intimidated by the head of the whole Academy."

"Nervous, yeah. On guard. But not scared. Don't make him scared. He's a lot sharper than this guy. He should act like it."

I'm not sure what to do. I feel like if I let Jonathan do this once, I can't say no the next time.

On the other hand, I do like his idea.

I try it his way.

It's better.

Finally he says, "Okay, let's stop."

I'm at the door leading to the stairwell when I realize Jonathan's not with me. I look back. He's standing by the wall, looking out at the river.

"You coming?"

He glances over. Then shakes his head. "Nah. I'm going to hang here for a while." His breath makes a cloud in the air, like he's smoking with no cigarette.

"It's just a little cold." Now that I'm not thinking in the game, I realize it really feels like January. I pull my arms in tight, hunch down in my jacket, and hop from foot to foot.

"I don't mind."

Doesn't he want to go home? I wonder. I mean, it's almost dinnertime.

Then I think of dinner at the Heitman house. Maybe not.

He's got to be cold, standing there by the wall. The wind's blowing right in his face.

I really should get back. My mom will be home soon. But it feels really creepy just to leave.

Letting the door slam shut, I walk over to the wall. Since I don't want Jonathan to feel like he has to talk to me, I stand nearby, but looking away from the river.

Once you're near the wall, it's a little warmer. The wind doesn't cut so sharp. Jonathan gets a cigarette out of his pocket. He's not looking at me, but he doesn't seem to mind I'm still here. As long as we're facing opposite directions, it's not like we're hanging out.

After a while I say, "It's definitely a cool view," meaning the water tower.

"Oh, yeah?"

"Sure." I look at him. "Don't you think?"

"Never done it."

"Oh." I nod once as he strikes a match under his palm. I can't believe he admitted he's never done it. "Well, you'll have to try it sometime and see."

He narrows his eyes, like he's trying to spot something across the river. Or like he's trying to imagine climbing up the water tower.

It's weird not to talk. But none of the things you would usually talk about seem like they would mean anything to Jonathan Heitman.

School? Who cares?

Parents? Who cares?

All that's left is movies or TV. And somehow I don't think we're into the same stuff.

For a second I wonder what that would be like: not to care about anything. Part of me admits: It would be kind of cool.

"So, what's it like?"

It takes me a second to understand Jonathan actually asked me something.

"What?"

"The whole Connolly thing. Is everyone there, like, a genius, or is it a lot of rich kids?"

"Uh, both. Most of the kids are pretty smart. And the

rest of them have half a brain." I think of Katie Mitchell. "Even if they pretend they don't."

"Yeah, right." He pitches the cigarette off the roof. "They just pretend to be stupid rich kids on Daddy's dime."

"You think everybody at Connolly is rich?"

"I bet more rich than actually intelligent."

"I'm not rich." I don't know why I feel like I have to say that; Jonathan should know I'm not. But I guess I want to make sure. Yeah, my dad does pay for it, but it's the only thing he pays for. According to my mom, anyway.

Jonathan shrugs. Like it doesn't matter if I am or I'm not; I go to school with those kids, so I might as well be one of them.

"Well, what's your school?" I ask, thinking how I could say, "Isn't that just a place for kids who are too screwed up even to pretend they're smart?"

He rolls his eyes, as if it couldn't matter less what his school is. What any school is. "What do you think?"

I say, "But they make you wear uniforms."

"The tie sucks. The rest of it, who cares?"

I wait, but that's all he says about it. I expected him to be more pissed off about the uniform thing, or at least want to tell me about how much he hates it.

I'd be horrified if they ever made me wear one. Skirts every day. I couldn't handle it. My brain would just rebel, switch off.

I say, "I couldn't do it."

He glances over. "Yeah, you in a skirt would be pretty hilarious. You could deal with the rest of it, though."

"What, like, prayers?"

"No, not that. I meant the school stuff. Grades. Academics. The things you have to be smart for."

I don't know why, but this annoys me. From Jonathan "smart" is probably an insult.

"You don't know I'm smart," I say. "You just think that because everyone's like, 'Oh, Judith, she's smart, she goes to Connolly.' It's like people say . . ."

That you're a jerk. That you're a drug addict.

"Besides," I say, "you're smart. You could do the whole school thing. If you wanted."

But Jonathan shakes his head. "There's different kinds of intelligence. There's school, that's smart. Then there's creativity, and that's . . . brightness. Being bright. I'm that. And then there's intelligent, which is kind of like the two combined. I'm only somewhat intelligent. Very few people are all three. You're all three."

People always say things like that to me. "You're smart." Or, "You're this."

But this is the first time it's ever felt like a compliment.

Because I feel like what he's saying is, *You may go to school with them, but you're not one of them.* Which is a little bit how I feel sometimes.

Then he says, "Your mom'll be home soon."

I look at my watch. Six thirty. He's right. She will be. Another test: Say, "I don't care," or "God, I got to go."

"What'd you tell her?" He looks at the water tower. "The other night?"

He wants to know if he's a secret. What I can't tell is does he want to be or not? "Nothing."

He nods.

Then I say, "I should go."

He says, "Cool."

I leave the wall, start walking to the door. I should be worried about my mom getting home before me. But in my head, like a jackhammer, is: Askdon'task. Askdon'task. Askdon'task. . . .

Somehow I feel like I can't leave until I know when this is happening again.

If it's happening again.

I get to the door, look back at Jonathan. He looks like I've already gone.

I want to say, "See you," but I know that's just asking for a promise.

So instead I don't say anything. Just go.

I do get home before my mom. Ten minutes before. When she comes through the door, I have my homework out, like I've been home for hours.

But I have to think of something. Some way to get out of the house after school.

"Surprise!" Is there anything worse you can hear at nine o'clock in the morning?

Particularly when the person with the surprise is Mr.

Jarman, who is even now writing our doom upon the white board.

JARMAN JEOPARDY DAY!

Then he turns to face us. "Jarman Jeopardy Day! Where everybody buzzes in and everybody answers!"

Everyone in the class just looks at him like, *Shoot me now.*

I am furious. Seriously angry.

What happened to voluntary participation? What happened to choice?

Yes, I went through the entire semester without speaking up. But I don't think we need to do this.

Then Mr. Jarman explains how Jarman Jeopardy Day works. "What happens is this. I write out the problem, you get three minutes to solve it." He holds up an hourglass egg timer. "Oh, and don't bother raising your hand. I'm going to be calling on people this time around."

He sets the hourglass on the desk.

This is torture. It's hell. I bet it's illegal. If it's not, it should be.

I mean, with so little time, nobody's going to get the answer right.

And I'm not the only one who thinks this. Michael Ruddick raises his hand, says, "So basically we're all going to bomb out."

Jarman smiles—I'm starting to hate his smile. "You guys have to get comfortable making mistakes. Take some risks. You're so worried you'll open your mouth, something wrong will come out, and the world will end."

For a split second he looks at me. "Okay? So everyone tries, everyone screws up. No risks and no wrong turns means no great mathematical minds."

He turns around, starts writing a problem on the board.

I think the last time I threw up in public was at the circus. I think I was five, and I felt stupid even then.

Mr. Jarman finishes writing. He calls the first name.

Then the next. And the next.

The first three people all get their problems wrong.

Think. Think. How can I get out of this?

Mr. Jarman? I have the Ebola virus. I need to see the nurse.

While I'm thinking about the likelihood of having Ebola, Neil McAlary screws up his problem. ("But good try, Neil," says Mr. Jarman. "Fascinating errors and miscalculations.")

Now Jarman's on the prowl, looking for his next victim.

Oh, God, not me.

Except it will be me sometime, so why not now? Get it over with. . . .

"David!" Mr. Jarman points to David Hofstra, then starts writing a problem on the board. David watches, real serious and focused. He loves this kind of stuff. Pressure, competition. Like when Michael Ruddick complained, David sneered, "What are you, a wuss-ass?"

Now he's stabbing the air with his pencil like he's

119

working a calculator. I think, Oh, please let him be wrong. It would be so sweet. . . .

But that's the ugly thing about this. You hope for kids to be wrong. Partly because some of them are jerks, like David, and partly so you won't be the only one. Like right now you can feel it: the whole class watching David, thinking, Be wrong, be wrong, be wrong. . . .

But David's not wrong. This time he gets it right. He hisses, "Yes!" and bangs his fist on the table.

Mr. Jarman smiles, congratulates David on the originality and depth of his thinking. "Okay, next . . ."

My stomach seizes up. Not me, not me, not me.

This time it's Michael Ruddick. He reacts by crossing his eyes and grinning maniacally. The whole class laughs. Even I laugh, because for the next three minutes I'm safe.

I do not see why we have to do this. I would have raised my hand eventually. Or Mr. Jarman could have just talked to me in private. He didn't have to put the whole class through this. I bet they're all pissed at me.

I don't mind making mistakes. I mean, I'd rather not. But . . . doing it in front of everyone else, with everybody watching. And you know they'll all think, "Duh, that was an easy one. She couldn't get that?"

I look at the clock. Wish really hard there were a way to make it leap forward to 3:30. That'd be so great, if life were like TiVo and you could just skip through the commercials and the annoying parts.

Maybe after college that's what I'll do. Become a scientist and work solely on time travel. Not only could you speed forward through things you knew were going to suck, you could also go back and change things. Make it so certain things in the past never took place. Think of all the people who'd still be alive, all the rotten things you could stop.

Actually, time has sped forward, and my three minutes of safety are up. Michael Ruddick gets the answer wrong. But he imitates David Hofstra, going "Yes!" and banging his fist on the table, and everyone laughs again. Except David.

And now Jarman's on the hunt again. And I don't know how I know, but I can feel it. . . .

It's going to be me.

My three minutes of hell are now.

"Ju-dith!" Jarman points.

If I were Michael Ruddick, I'd say, "Jar-man," and everyone would laugh and it wouldn't matter if I got the answer right or wrong.

Only, my throat feels like I just swallowed a bucket of sand, so I can't.

Stare at the board, stare at the board. Nowhere else. Forget everything else. Nobody's watching. Nobody's here. . . .

My heart's going a million beats a minute. I'm looking at the problem and I don't have the first clue how to solve it.

So, who cares? Jarman says it doesn't matter if you get it wrong, so just . . . get it wrong.

But I can't. I can't. . . .

Take the first part, work it through.

My brain starts moving again. The numbers look a little less like Sanskrit. I get the first part, then move on and . . .

And I am completely lost.

I can feel that stupid little timer. The sand seeping through. I start thinking about Dorothy and the Wizard of Oz. . . .

Quit it! Look at the problem.

Okay. Okay. Deep breath. Take the result of the first part, hold it in your head. Then the second part. How do they work together? They do, you just have to figure out how.

I am going to get this so wrong.

In a neutral voice Jarman says, "Minute to go."

And that does something to my brain, because it just takes over like a weird calculator gone berserk. I can see the problem, numbers moving around, falling into place.

Jarman raises his hand. "And . . ."

I give the answer.

There's a long pause. I notice the class again; they're all looking at Jarman.

Who says, "Correct, Ms. Ellis."

For the rest of the class I'm in such a daze of relief I almost forget to leave. Then I notice everyone filing out and scramble out of my seat. I concentrate on getting everything into my bag because I don't want to see anyone.

Particularly Mr. Jarman.

But when I get to the door, I hear, "Ms. Ellis?"

I stop and glance back. Mr. Jarman's tidying up the stuff on his desk. For a second I think I imagined hearing my name.

Then he says, "Now that that's over with"—he smiles—"I wonder if you would think about something."

I almost smile. Jarman's so weird, the way he talks. "Sure."

"I'd like you to think about tutoring."

Tutoring? I don't know what I thought he was going to ask me, but I didn't think it would be this.

"What, like, kids from Connolly?"

"A kid from Connolly."

"Who?"

"No" is my immediate answer. Connolly kids can buy their own tutors, they don't need me.

But Mr. Jarman's never asked me to do anything before. Nobody has. And for Mr. Jarman to say, *I want you to do this* . . .

You'd have to be a loser to say no.

Plus, if I'm honest about it, it's the perfect thing to get me out of the house to see Jonathan. *Hey, Mom, I'm going to be late. Gotta go do some tutoring.*

So I say, "Okay, sure. What do I have to do?"

"You have to . . ." He seems to notice for the first time that I'm on the other side of the room. He waves. "Come up here for a minute."

I go up to his desk. As I do I look back at the empty classroom, wonder what it would be like if everyone were here and I were the teacher. Terrifying, basically.

Mr. Jarman gets out a folder, shows me a sheet of paper with a list of math concepts on it. They look familiar; then I realize it's all the stuff I did last year.

Looking down at the folder, he says, "We have a young lady who is failing to thrive."

"What does that mean?"

He sighs. "It means she didn't do very well on her last two tests. It means she needs to do much, much better on her final. She's already working with her teacher, Ms. Isaacs. But we thought another student could be helpful too." He looks at me. "Sometimes people need a reason to make the effort."

"What kind of reason?" I want to ask. But before I can, Jarman hands me the folder. "Anyway, her phone number's inside. Why don't you give her a call tonight, see when she'd like to meet."

I take the folder. "What happens if she doesn't do well on the final?"

"If she doesn't do well on the final, she may not be coming back to Connolly next year."

For a second I want to give the folder back. I only started this so I could have an excuse to get out of the house to see Jonathan. Now it's going to be up to me if someone flunks out or not.

I open the folder to see who the mystery guest is.

Katie Mitchell.

TWELVE

I can't believe this.

I cannot believe it.

I'm supposed to help Katie Mitchell pass math? Katie "Ha, Ha, I'm Brain-dead" Mitchell? The girl whose parents probably paid for her to get in?

I can't talk her out of thinking she's stupid. I think she is totally stupid.

I'm halfway down the hall when I think I should just give the dumb folder back to Jarman. Go back and tell him, "I'm sorry, but no."

I actually do turn around.

But in the end I can't do it.

Because it's kind of like the ladder. Once you step on the first rung, you have to keep going.

Even if you think it's going to be a major disaster.

At least it'll give me a cover for Jonathan if I need it.

At least my mom'll be happy.

My mom is even more out of her mind with happiness than I thought she would be. At dinner she keeps saying over and over how great it is, how fantastic. The more gonzo she gets, the more overwhelmed I feel. Like, You think I can help this chick? Yeah, right. Think again.

Finally, because I can't take it anymore, I say, "I'm not so sure if I can help Katie—"

My mom interrupts. "Of course you can. Why do you think you can't?"

"She's kind of an airhead. She thinks it's embarrassing if she admits she has a brain."

"Maybe no one ever told her she did have one. Or . . ." My mom thinks. "Some people are scared that if they're smart once, they'll have to start being smart all the time. That's a lot of work. If you're dumb, nobody expects anything from you."

I pick over my food. "I hate it when girls do that."

"When girls do what?"

"Act all . . ." I toss my head from side to side like there's a pea rolling around in it. In a high voice I say, "'I'm so dumb. I don't have a clue.'"

"Girls do this, huh." I can tell from my mom's voice

she doesn't agree with me. Which is weird because I thought she might. I know she gets really angry whenever someone suggests women can't do everything men can.

She waves her fork at me. "Boys never do that. They never act dumb."

I'm not sure what my mom wants me to say here. "Sometimes they are dumb. . . ."

"Whereas every single girl, all over the world," she says, "acts dumb all the time."

"I didn't say that." Even though I do sort of think of it as something girls do, and I'm annoyed that my mom is pretending she has no clue what I'm talking about. "I didn't say all girls all the time. . . ."

I'm really frustrated my mom doesn't get this.

I crumple up my napkin and throw it on the table.

After a moment she smiles. "I know what you mean, honey. Just watch those wild, swinging accusations of yours. There's . . . nothing wrong with being a girl, you know."

My mom's still smiling, but there's something in her eyes that makes me sad. It's like she thinks there's something really wrong with me.

I want to ask her, "Do you think I'm totally strange?"

But I'm afraid of what she'll say.

After dinner I get out the folder and pick up the phone.

It's been a while since I called anyone. I forgot how it can be scary. You dial up, and all of a sudden there's this person there, and you're like, Okay, now what do I say?

Mrs. Taplow? Hi, it's Judith.

Oh, hi, Mrs. Taplow. Is Leia home?

Hey, Leia, I guess you're not picking up, but . . . it's me, and call me, okay?

Quickly I punch in the numbers for Katie. As it starts to ring I wonder who answers the phone in her house.

At first I think I have the wrong number, because the first voice I hear doesn't sound like Katie's mom, unless Katie's mom is from the Caribbean, which I don't think she is.

Then I hear another *click* and Katie saying, "It's okay, Marie, I got it, thanks. Hello?"

"Uh, hi . . . it's Judith. Ellis. From school."

"Oh, hi." Katie sounds friendly, but surprised. "Wow, what's up?"

"I was, uh, talking to Mr. Jarman? And he said that you . . ." I'm about to say "needed," but that sounds obnoxious. "Wanted a tutor? For math?"

There's a long pause. Oh, God, I blew it.

"So, wait," Katie says slowly. "Are you going to be my tutor? Oh, my God."

She starts laughing hysterically.

I say, "What?"

"No, I mean, it's cool. I was worried they were going to send me some yawn-o-rama nerd boy. But this'll be totally fun."

Fun? Somehow I don't think Katie quite gets the idea.

Then Katie says, "So, when do you want to come over?"

Katie's house isn't far from school. You can tell her parents are the kind of people who don't go ten blocks beyond their house. Except maybe to the airport. And then only in a cab.

I heard that that's how Katie gets to school every morning. Her parents give her money for a cab because they don't want her taking the bus or subway.

In the lobby of Katie's building the doorman stops me and asks who I want to see.

I say, "Katie Mitchell?"

He picks up the intercom phone, presses a button on the panel. "Who may I say is calling?"

I say, "Judith Ellis," just as I hear a crackle and "Hello?" from the other side.

The doorman says, "Judith Ellis to see you."

There's a pause. Then he puts the phone back on the hook.

"Nine C," he says, and points to the elevator.

There are cameras in the elevator. And even a little screen so you can watch yourself being watched.

I think: Jonathan's lucky we don't have those in our building.

When I get out of the elevator, the first thing I notice is the complete silence. There's wall-to-wall carpet, and even cloth on the walls. It's like being inside one of those padded jewelry boxes.

I go to 9C, ring the bell. After a second the peephole opens. I half wave.

The door opens wide.

Katie says, "Hey! Come in!"

Katie's place is enormous. And I think Katie and I are the only ones here—until I hear a vacuum cleaner, and I realize Marie is around too.

We go into the kitchen, where Katie gets out soda and popcorn. All over the refrigerator there're these obnoxious magnets. Things like little pigs saying, "Don't pig out!" And the Slim Support emergency number.

Katie catches me looking and says, "Mom's reminders."

I think, Gross. But since I can't say that, I ask her, "So, are you an only?"

"Yep." She grins. "Guess my parents figured, God, one was bad enough."

Okay, one thing we have in common. "Me too. I kind of like it."

Katie concentrates on pouring the soda. "Yeah . . ." Then she smiles. "Who wants to share, right?"

She sits down, reaches for a handful of popcorn. "So, what do you want to do?"

Want to do? I put the folder Mr. Jarman gave me on the table. "Uh, maybe we could start with quadratics?"

I try to say it like it's fun—*Hey, quadratics!* But Katie looks less than thrilled.

She says, "Let's go hang in my room."

Katie's room is immaculate. It feels like a model room, not a place anyone lives. You just . . . buy it.

There are no posters on the walls. The TV is on, but the sound's off. On the screen some women are waving shoes around. A few photographs in clear frames on the windowsill. I look. Katie and her mom. Katie and her dad. Katie lying on the floor, petting a sleeping cat.

"That's Monty," she says. "He died last year."

"Sorry."

She shrugs. "He was twelve years old, he had an okay life. But he started peeing everywhere, and my dad was like . . ." She makes a cutting gesture across her throat.

"That's harsh." I don't know what else to say. Killing a cat because he's old seems really mean to me. But you can't say, "Oh, so your dad's a jerk."

"Yeah." Katie sighs, then looks around the floor, like she expects Monty to come crawling out from underneath the bed.

"Hey." I go over to her desk, where she has this sleek flat-screen computer. "Cool computer. This is the new one, right?"

I tap the space bar. The computer purrs to life. A big house without a roof appears on the screen.

"Oh, hey," says Katie happily, "are you into *Sims*? I am totally hooked."

She points to a woman in a miniskirt and leather jacket watering flowers in the garden. "That's my Sim. Clarissa Le Fey."

I say, "Clarissa has a big house for one little Sim."

"Oh, no, she's got this enormo family. They drive her crazy. Never give her any privacy." She clicks again, and a mom and dad start walking around in the house. "Plus, of course, her many suitors, such as Nick Nice Guy."

Then Katie gives me this sly smile. "Clarissa did have a

best friend. Two best friends. But they met with a tragic accident in the swimming pool. Mwah-ah-ah . . ."

She cackles in this totally macabre way. I'm shocked; I've never seen this side of her. "Evil Katie." I kind of like it.

She catches the expression on my face, starts shutting down the computer. "You probably think this is totally sad, right? Like, 'Hi, Lame Girl lives in Fantasy World.'"

"No, not at all."

"I mean, it is lame. But I like it, you know? Your own little world. You take them shopping, make them go to the bathroom, have them fight. I don't know. They're fun."

I nod. My fantasy would never be shopping or drowning people. But I totally get what Katie means about your own little world.

And frankly, if my house were as empty as hers is, I'd fill it up with anybody I could. Even Sims.

I say, "Reality's pretty overrated."

Now it's Katie's turn to be surprised. She laughs. "Completely. I give it a C minus."

"D plus."

We both laugh a little. Then I say, "So, look, where do you want to start with the math stuff?"

Katie sighs, flops down on her bed. "Look, can I admit something to you?"

"Sure."

"I only said I'd have a tutor so everyone would stop yelling at me. I mean, every day Ms. Isaacs was like, 'You have to have a tutor. Let me tutor you.' So I said yes. And then they were like, 'How about another student? Would that help you? Someone who sees it from your perspective?' And I was like, 'Okay, fine.' But I might as well just tell you now. I'm totally going to flunk."

"Why?"

"Because I'm stupid." She says it right out, like *Because I have red hair.* "I know everyone says it: 'Oh, Katie, she's just at Connolly because Mommy and Daddy gave all this money to the school.' And you know what? They're right."

"Really?"

She shrugs. "Basically."

It's funny. I always thought if the rumor about Katie was true, I could never like her, because it's skeevy to get in on your parents' money.

Now that I know it is true, I just feel sorry for her. It's not her fault. She didn't ask her parents to do it.

Maybe that's why she's screwing up. Because she hates Connolly and wants out. Particularly after getting dumped by K&J.

I ask her, "Do you want to flunk?"

Katie picks at the bedspread. "No. Just . . . I don't really feel like I belong there most of the time, you know?"

I think about that. Because maybe she doesn't. Maybe she isn't smart enough.

But she can't be any stupider than K&J. And shouldn't niceness count for something? Or . . . funniness? Why does everyone have to be the Best?

I say, "I think you should try and stay. I'm willing to give it a shot."

Katie smiles, shakes her head. "I will seriously frustrate you. I frustrate everybody."

"I frustrate most people too."

"I don't get any of the things I'm supposed to understand."

"Me neither."

"And people usually end up telling me to get lost."

"Me too."

There's another, very long pause. Katie says, "Then, I guess . . ."

"Yeah?"

She grins. "Well, it could be interesting to see who tells who to get lost first."

In the end we don't do any math. Katie takes Clarissa shopping for bedroom furniture instead. Then she kills off the saleslady by having her get hit by a car.

She says, "I hate snotty salesladies, don't you?"

I say, "I kind of hate the whole shopping thing in general."

Katie looks surprised. Then says, "That's cool."

When I get home, my mom wants to hear all about how it went. I say, "Well, as far as math goes . . . ," and put my thumb down. "But in other ways it was all right."

My mom asks what that means, but since I'm not sure, I shrug and say I'll tell her later. It was kind of fun hanging with Katie. But I think I want to hear silence for a while.

When I check my e-mail, I see I have a message.

It says, **2/03. 1630. 13th floor.**

It's funny how you can go along thinking everything's okay, it's life and you're there, and no big deal.

And then something happens and you realize that wasn't life at all.

After dinner I don't have much homework. My mom's working in her study, so the TV is free. It was my dad who finally made us get cable. My mom fought it forever, saying things like, "A hundred channels, and still nothing I want to watch." Now she says cable's the only place with anything good on.

Flicking through the channels, I think she might have been right the first time.

I don't want the news and I hate reality shows, so I end up watching this movie about some girl who's supposed to be so smart and edgy and unpopular. She wears glasses, that's how you know she's so smart. And she's the only one that has dark hair in the school—a place that looks like Planet Blond.

Anyway, she somehow ends up going to the prom—hello, gag—and she doesn't wear her glasses, so suddenly she's all beautiful. And she's bashful and shy because she doesn't feel comfortable wearing a dress. But then the guy says something like, "Wow, I never knew you were so pretty," and she feels on top of the world.

So, basically, the whole point is she's pretty. Oh, and

smart, too. But what's really important here is that she's pretty.

For a second I think about Katie. About her thin little Clarissa Le Fey.

It must be a pain being fat. There are *no* fat people on Planet Blond.

I don't get it. I mean, even movies where the actress is smart—like they seem like they'd be smart in real life, they're not just wearing glasses for the movie—even they're all gorgeous. And they usually get a boyfriend somewhere in the story. Even if they say they don't want one. They always, always end up falling in love, and you're supposed to be like, "Oh, thank God."

I once said this to my mom, and she laughed. "Honey, Hollywood . . . reality—two different universes. Don't make yourself crazy."

Which made me feel pretty pathetic. Like I didn't know the difference between a movie and the real world.

But then when everyone gets on you about your hair and your clothes and your this and your that, and "Are you fat?" and "Are you sexy?" you start thinking, Hey, maybe I'm not the only one who can't tell the difference between movies and reality.

Maybe everyone really does think you can look like that. And that you should look like that.

Because, you know, otherwise you might not get to go to the prom and fall in love.

THIRTEEN

It's 4:37.

And it's raining.

Like, really raining.

I'm standing on the roof at the base of the tower, huddled against the wall, banging my feet on the tar to keep them from freezing. I'd walk around, but the wind and rain would probably knock me over.

Where is Jonathan? The game is ready to go in my head. It's driving me crazy.

Gareth waited for Evans in the usual spot. . . .

Ugh. No. Start again.

Endurance mattered. And so every winter the cadets were marched out to a frozen field and . . .

Shot, I don't know. I'm kind of wishing someone would shoot me. I'm so cold and wet I don't think I'd even feel it.

What time is it? Four forty-five.

I'll wait until five. After that, he can't expect me to be here.

Evans has no expectations of anyone, thought Gareth. Or rather: only one. That they would do what he told them to. Unthinkingly and without question.

Of course, Jonathan may not be coming at all. He might have seen the rain and decided, Screw it. Not worth it.

My teeth are chattering so hard I feel like they're going to fall out.

Maybe waiting inside the stairwell isn't the worst idea.

But just as I get to the door that leads to the stairwell it opens.

Jonathan.

He stares at me. I guess with the rain I look a little strange.

"You're actually here," he says.

"Where else would I be?"

He looks up at the sky. "Little wet."

I look where he's looking. "Yeah."

Then I say, "But I have an idea about that."

Usually when someone comes to your place, you ask if they want a soda or something. But Jonathan goes straight to my room like it's the only safe place in the house.

For a second he paces around. Then he stops. "You sure about this? 'Cause your mom would have a freak attack, and I'm not in the mood."

I shrug. "Well, she's not here to have a freak attack, so . . ."

He nods, sits down at the desk. "Okay—here's where we are. The governor has told Evans to quit meeting one-on-one with a student; gives Gareth an inflated sense of who he is—kid's just going to be cannon fodder anyway. Why waste the time on him?"

"What does Evans say?"

Jonathan widens his eyes. "Well, you'll see."

For a second he sits quietly in my desk chair. You can almost see Evans's office appearing around him. Then he says abruptly, "Come in."

I take a step forward. Carefully.

"I hear you met with our esteemed governor." I nod. "I'm sure he told you not to tell anyone what was said at that meeting." I nod again. "Will you tell me?"

"Of course."

"What did he say?"

"That you were dangerous. That I shouldn't trust you."

"You shouldn't."

"He said your students tend to be accident prone."

Jonathan/Evans smiles. "And what did you say to him?"

"That I won't tell you."

"Of course not." He turns in the chair, looks toward the window, so I can't see his face. "You are what we call a promising candidate. I was once a promising candidate. Do you know what happens to promising candidates?"

"No."

Jonathan swings back. "They become proconsuls—or they have accidents. Do you know why?"

I think. "Because there can be only so many proconsuls. And the ones that exist don't want to be replaced before their time."

Jonathan nods. "Very promising."

Then he stands up. "Now get out. This was our last meeting."

This actually surprises me. The question comes naturally. "Why?"

Jonathan's face is blank. "I don't explain myself to you."

As Gareth, I think: *Why call me into his office to call off the meetings? Why not cancel? Why tell me I'm a promising candidate and then stop treating me as one?*

Because promising candidates replace proconsuls?

Or because promising candidates have accidents?

Is Evans protecting me or throwing me to the wolves?

Jonathan's face doesn't give me a clue.

"What time does your mom get home?"

It's funny Jonathan asks that. We've been talking about totally different stuff—school, Dalmas, whatever. But for a little while now I've been wondering how I can tell him that he should probably leave because my mom'll be home soon. And wondering how long I can wait before I do.

He's sitting at my desk, holding on to the edge of it while he turns himself slowly in my chair. You can make yourself dizzy doing that.

I'm sitting on my bed, and it's like two little islands.

"Around six thirty usually."

He nods, and I can tell he's decided: Leave in a few minutes.

Then he looks at the window. "You do have a very cool view."

I glance over my shoulder. The rain has finally stopped, and it's totally dark out. All over the city the lights are going on.

Getting off the bed, I heave the window open, push up the screen. "If you look all the way out, you can see, like . . . everything."

Jonathan gets up, comes to the window. I step back so he has room to lean out. Stretching to see, he whistles.

I think for a second, then say, "Hold on. . . ."

I go to the light switch, turn off the lights. Now the only thing you can see is Jonathan and the window.

Jonathan says, "Great." But he's leaning out the window, and it's like he's outside. His hair's whipping around in the wind.

There's room for me to lean out too. But instead I lean against the wall inside. Jonathan rests his elbows on the ledge outside.

"Ever see anything in those windows?" He points to some buildings across the street.

I look. "Yeah, sometimes."

"Yeah? Like what?"

"Oh . . ." I haven't actually seen anything that wild, and now I have to think of something impressive. To gain time, I lean out the window, making sure I'm not brushing up against him or anything.

Now we're both outside, and I have to speak up a little to be heard.

"You know. The usual. Like, I once saw a guy naked."

"Where?"

"Uh, there . . ." I point to one of the windows.

"Huh." Either Jonathan's not that interested or he doesn't believe me. He points to the movie theater across the street. "That's cool, you always know what's on."

"Yeah." I nod, like I check the movies all the time.

Then I say, "You're a good actor."

He looks surprised. "Thanks."

"No, really. It's like . . ." I think of Jonathan turning away from me in the chair. "I forget you're you."

He nods. "Yeah, sometimes I forget too. About you."

I want to ask what he means, what it is that he forgets. But then he points. "Oh, hey. You can see Eric's."

"What?" I look where he's pointing.

"This bar, a guy called Eric runs it. Me and my dad go sometimes."

I don't know what to say. Mr. Heitman is not something I know how to talk about with Jonathan. It feels dangerous. Like say the wrong thing—something too nice or too mean or just stupid—and he could lose it. And yet he talks about him in this totally bored voice, like he couldn't care less.

"Is it interesting?"

"Depends. Sometimes it's okay. Sometimes it blows. When he's hammered, my dad has a tendency to talk. One minor problem: He doesn't make any sense. So you can spend a lot of time going, 'Um-hm, yeah, right,' when you wish he'd just shut up."

I laugh, and he looks at me. I feel weird, like I just admitted something.

"No, sometimes," I say, "my dad—he's in Seattle—when he calls, it's the same thing. He always asks the same questions over and over, and as long as you fill in the blank, it's cool." I go robotic. "'I am fine. How are you?'"

Jonathan laughs. "Yeah. Could be anybody, as long as they say the right thing."

For a little while we watch the people below, so far away they're not even real. I try to find Eric's again. I forget about touching. I mean, Jonathan's right there, but it's no big thing. It's kind of nice that it isn't.

Then I hear, "I should go."

He pulls himself back inside, and after a second I do too, shut the window, and flick on the light.

As he's picking up his coat he looks over at my atomic bomb poster like he's trying to figure out why I have it up there, so I say, "My great-uncle helped build it."

"Seriously?"

"Well, him and about a thousand other people, but yeah."

He steps closer to the poster. "Does look sort of cool."

I look at the cloud. People always call it a mushroom, but it feels more like an umbrella to me. Except whatever's underneath it isn't protected, it's gone. Destroyed.

And probably no one even saw it coming. Like one minute there's life, everything's normal and boring, and then it's . . . over. I don't think those people even knew what was happening; how could they? I guess it's better not to know. You'd go crazy knowing.

You can definitely go crazy thinking about it. How everything that you think is could just not be one day. In a matter of seconds, totally wiped out.

Jonathan says, "That's cool about your uncle."

He goes to the door. "So, look. You want to say Friday? For next time?"

"Yeah, sure."

"Here."

"Yeah."

He leaves. A few seconds later I hear the front door shut.

Afterward the room feels so horribly empty I sit on my bed and put my headphones on. I can imagine a lot of different scenes when I'm listening to music. It's neat how music makes the world go away. Lets another world take shape.

I'm trying to imagine what Gareth does after the scene with Evans, when out of the corner of my eye I see my door open, my mom's face peering through the crack. . . .

I tear off the headphones. Stare at her. Coming into my room without knocking is absolutely not allowed. She knows that.

She says, "I knocked . . . you couldn't hear."

Then, you should have just gone away, I think, and come back later. Even though I wasn't doing anything, I feel embarrassed. Sometimes when I listen to music, I get up, act stuff out. . . .

The thought of my mother seeing that makes me nauseous.

I can feel it, she wants me to apologize to her. For tuning her out. Yeah, God forbid, Ma, I can never not hear you.

"Those things are terrible for your hearing," she says about the headphones.

"I don't have them on loud."

"Well . . ." My mom laughs a little, then doesn't say what I know she wants to: *Obviously they're too loud if you can't hear me.*

Somehow it feels like we're fighting, even though neither of us wants to be. For a moment no one says anything.

Then my mom says, "I just ran into Mrs. Heitman in the elevator."

"Oh, yeah?" Neutral. Like no big deal.

"She told me how pleased she was."

I have no idea what my mom's talking about, so I smile crookedly, like, *Okay, nice, but weird*.

"That you and Jonathan are becoming friends."

"Oh."

"I felt sort of silly. I . . . didn't know you two were friends."

"Yeah, we're kind of." I shrug. "I mean, I don't know."

"Well, his mom seems to think he's seeing you a lot."

"I wouldn't say a lot."

"She says he's over here a lot."

I'm about to say something about how Mrs. Heitman is probably thrilled that Jonathan has any friends at all, when my mom blurts out, "I don't see how you can have time, with classes and now your tutoring job. I mean, is this still about school? Giving your notes or . . ."

It's a stupid question, but she's come closer to the bed, like the answer's really important to her, and I better give her the right one or else.

I stammer, "No. No . . . but . . ."

"Then, why is he over here?"

"I don't know. We hang out, we talk. It's not a big thing, Ma."

She steps closer to me. She's trying to keep it together, but it's not working entirely, which makes me scared. "Just tell me."

"Tell you what?"

"I think you know."

"No, I am a little clueless here," I say.

She takes a final step toward the bed, and I know my mom would never, ever hit me, but for a second it feels like she's going to, she's that mad.

I shout, "We are not doing drugs, okay?" Because I'm really pissed off that I would ever have to say that to my mother. That she wouldn't know that about me.

She steps back a moment. Good, I freaked her out this time. Whoever's talking definitely has the advantage here, so I keep going. "Is that what you wanted to know? Because if it was, we're not. I mean, I don't know what Jonathan does. But I'm . . . not."

I look at her. "Okay?"

She raises her hands. Whispers, "Yeah, okay."

She goes back to the door, takes hold of the knob. For a moment she stares at it. Then she turns her head to look back at me. "I just didn't think you liked him that much."

"He can be okay."

"Yeah, he can also be a real problem." She sighs. "I just don't want . . ." She looks back at the doorknob, like it's going to make more sense to her than I am right now.

I say, "I know what you don't want. And it's not happening."

Without looking at me, she nods. Then she opens the door with one jerk of her arm and closes it the same way. It slams shut. I don't think she meant to slam it. But she did.

For a few minutes I just sit there. I think of all the things my mom thinks could be happening. All the images she has in her head. I don't know, me lighting up, me . . .

necking, or something, I don't know. And I keep wondering, Why does she think these things about me? How could she ever think I'm that person?

Like the only possible reason a male and female would converse is to . . .

Hi, Mom, maybe you didn't notice, but I'm not that kind of girl? Like, really not that kind?

The thing is, I don't think my mom would be any happier if I told her what was really going on. She'd probably be more freaked than ever.

I wish I could explain to her what it felt like sitting on that roof waiting for Jonathan to come and thinking he wasn't going to show. Like nothing would ever happen again. And then what it felt like to see him at the door and know it was a mistake, that I hadn't been blown off, that . . .

That he wanted to see me, too.

I mean, not see me. But that the game's important to me, and it's also important to him.

And that when you're slightly weird, nobody ever seems to give a crap about the things that are important to you.

So when you find someone who gets it . . .

Whatever that is—that's what I wish I could explain to her.

FOURTEEN

One thing I realize: If I'm going to tutor Katie, I have to be better prepared.

Because you go over there, and the next thing you know, you're hanging out, watching TV, or playing *Sims*. You keep thinking, Okay, next commercial, we're going to start working.

But it never happens.

Basically, Katie is very good at not doing what she doesn't want to do.

I can tell part of her doesn't want to fail. Part of her doesn't want to be the dumb rich girl whose parents paid to get her into Connolly. But I think it freaks her out, too.

I mean, what happens if you try not to be the doof everyone says you are, but you find out, whoops, you really are a doof?

You probably think, Screw it. Zap on the TV.

Which is why I have to get serious. Which is why I'm going to the library during my free period, so I can study the next chapter in Katie's math book and figure out a way to get her psyched about algebra.

Only, there's one thing I forget.

The library is Leia's territory.

Something I remember the second I walk through the door and get the Look of Death from Leia, who is sitting right there.

It's a very little Look of Death. Maybe a split second before she picks up her notebook and stares at it, as if hypnotized.

This is Leia's other favorite weapon: the Invisiblizer.

Kelsey, who's sitting next to her, sticks with the Look of Death.

Part of me just wants to turn around and walk right out.

Then I think, No. Just because she's here doesn't mean I can't be here. I mean, it's not like she's radioactive.

I try to find a seat far away from them. But unfortunately the library's really crowded, and there's nowhere else for me to sit except at their table.

As I sit down I hear them whisper to each other. But I turn on my own Invisiblizer and try to figure out how I can make algebra fun to someone who gags at the sight of numbers.

I open Katie's math book, start taking notes.

A few minutes later I hear it. The slide of a notebook.

I happen to know from past experience: Sharing a notebook is Leia's favorite way of passing notes. It looks like you're working, but all you're doing is scribbling stuff about other people.

Right now the notebook's zooming back and forth. I glance over at Ms. Zbriskie, the librarian, but she's busy helping someone.

I pretend I don't hear. Turn the page.

But it's hard. Little things slip through. Like the scratch of a pen, really fast, like the person can't wait to get it all down.

Then Kelsey whispers, "No, wait . . ."

More scratching. The notebook slides. Then Leia laughs.

Even Ms. Zbriskie hears it and says, "Leia? Kelsey?" Nice, but with a little warning.

She starts heading this way. I hear paper being torn, then crumpled up. A little crunch as it drops to the floor. Leia always hides the evidence.

Ms. Zbriskie tells Leia and Kelsey that if they want to talk, they can go outside.

A few seconds later I hear Kelsey whisper, "Do you want to just go?"

And Leia, "Yeah, I think I do." In that breathy, tired way

she does when she wants you to think she's sick so you'll do something for her.

So they split.

But they leave the stupid piece of paper behind.

Right there on the floor.

I should just ignore it. Forget it exists. It has nothing to do with me.

Except I know that's not true. It has everything to do with me. It's about me.

It's not that far from my foot. All I have to do is bend down like I dropped my pen or something and pick it up.

But why should I?

Why do I care what Leia's saying, anyway?

I try to sit with that for a moment, really try to feel it: I don't care.

It doesn't work. I do care.

Or it's not so much that I care. It's just that I'm curious. Like, why is she still so bothered? Why does she care?

Okay, just take the stupid thing, because you know you're not leaving here without it.

The thing is, if it's really bad, I don't want anyone else reading it.

So I bend down. Find it. Take it.

Leia crumpled it up good and tight. I really have to pull to get it straightened out. At one point I tear the paper a little.

But not so much that I can't read it.

In Leia's handwriting: *I can't DEAL!!*

Then Kelsey's: *Pretend she doesn't exist. Give her NO satisfaction.*

A gap on the paper. Then from Leia: *Not working! She's freaking me out.*

I hear you, girlfriend.

God, it's like wherever I go, she's THERE!

Yeah, well, you know why.

At first I'm like, Yeah, okay, whatever. My brain says it could have been a lot worse. But my stomach doesn't agree. My stomach is one hard, twisted knot.

It's almost funny, how afraid Leia is of me.

Yeah, well, you know why.

No, Kelsey, I don't know why. Enlighten me.

I squeeze the stupid note in my hand. What I really want to do is hurl it in Leia's face.

Like, *You're scared of me?*

Then, be scared of me for real.

I slam Katie's textbook shut. No point. I can't concentrate.

In a few hours I'll see Jonathan. In a few hours I'll be someone else entirely.

And then who cares what Leia Taplow is saying about Judith Ellis?

Except Jonathan doesn't come at 4:30, like he's supposed to.

Not at 4:45. Or even 4:50.

In fact, when the doorbell finally does ring, it's after five o'clock.

153

No excuse, nothing. Instead he gives me this little look like, *Yeah, I know you're pissed off. So what?*

And for the first time since we started doing the game, I remember that I don't always like Jonathan Heitman.

When we go back to my room, he throws himself on the bed, heaves this huge sigh.

"So," he says, "what do you want to do?"

I sit up on the edge of my desk. "Uh, the game?" Sarcastic, but just a little.

Jonathan snorts at the ceiling. "Brilliant. What scene *in* the game?"

Okay. So he's tired of coming up with scenes. That's cool. But he could say it in a slightly less obnoxious way.

I say, "Why don't we do Gareth talking to one of the other cadets?"

Jonathan yawns.

"Or Evans meeting with—"

Jonathan snores.

"Yeah, okay," I snap. "You think of something."

Jonathan sits up, balances his chin on his fingers. "We need something new. A new character." He stands up. "It's gotten too predictable. Gareth, Evans. Too many guys. We need a woman."

"What kind of woman?"

"Like . . ." Jonathan narrows his eyes, thinking. "A wife. The wife of the Academy governor, maybe. Yeah. Everyone thinks because she's the wife of this high-ranking guy, she's all proper, but you don't really know what her agenda is, and that makes her dangerous."

He starts pacing again, like his head's so full he can't stop moving.

As he describes her I try to imagine it, what it'd be like to play this person.

"You assume that she's totally bought into the whole thing, but really she's looking for her own power base here. She's bored with her husband, because let's face it, he's a total loser—"

"And what?" I interrupt. "She's, like, wildly sexy and gorgeous?"

Jonathan's face is bland, you can't read it. "Kind of more interesting if she is."

I put on a fake soap-opera voice. "And she seduces man after man, deceiving them with her wiles, using her charms to get what she wants—namely, power and more power!"

I fall back on the desk, hoping Jonathan will get the joke and laugh. But when I sit up, he's perfectly serious.

"Basically," he says. "Problem?"

Only a million things—chiefly me. I'm not seeing me as this person. At. All. *Why, Evans, sit down. . . .* Gag.

I can play a lot of things, but not a megaseductress. Which Jonathan should know.

So why is he asking me to do it?

I wish he weren't in such a weird mood.

Finally I say, "I don't know if I can do this."

"What do you mean?"

"This character."

He steps in close. "Why not?"

"Because." I shrug. "It's not me."

"Oh. And Gareth is you."

"More than this one."

He narrows his eyes. "You do the governor, you do other characters you don't like. . . ."

"Okay, but not this one."

"Why not?" He stands right in front of me. "Why not?"

He leans in, puts his hands on either side of me on the desk. I feel a flare: *Get off.*

I say, "You think she's so great, you do her."

For a long moment we just look at each other.

Then he steps back. His hands fall away. He's going to leave, I'm convinced of it.

He says, "Cool. I will."

At first I think, No way. No way is this going to work. Because Jonathan's not just a guy, he's a guy. He's got a deep voice and this whole *Screw you* 'tude. The way he walks, the way he moves—it's just not how a girl walks and moves. I know, because I've tried to walk like him and I can't.

I bet in about five seconds he's embarrassed and says, "Forget it, let's do it the old way."

But he doesn't. First he does the voice, trying to find one that sounds like a woman but doesn't get all high and shrieky.

He clears his throat, says, "Hi." Then, "What do you think?"

I remember in the beginning how I was scared that he

would tell me, "Wrong, guys don't do that." So I don't tell him when he makes a mistake. Like when he flips his hair, I don't say, "Uh, have you ever seen me do that?"

"It's okay," I tell him.

In the first scene we do, I play her husband, the pompous Academy governor, and she tells me that she wants to give a dinner for the staff.

Jonathan says, "And you're suspicious because she's never shown any interest in that kind of thing before, why does she want to now?"

I'm playing the husband, so I feel like I should come on strong, be very bossy, and just tell her no. But somehow, the way Jonathan plays her, I can't do that. It's hard to pin her down. So instead I ask a lot of questions.

"I don't see why you want to go to all the trouble."

Jonathan frowns. "It's no trouble."

"All that work." I do a patronizing smile.

Jonathan smiles back. "I'll get other people to do that."

"But why?"

"I want to meet people. I want to know who everyone is." Jonathan pauses. "I want them to know me."

"They know you."

"They see me, it's not the same." Jonathan rubs my arm, stands close. "Please?"

It's exactly what his character would do. But I admit, I'm a little impressed when Jonathan actually does it. Something like that could get you laughed at. But Jonathan's so real you can't.

When I say she can have the dinner, it occurs to me

157

that I should kiss him on the cheek. A husband would, right?

But I don't know if I can do it as well as he did, and before I can decide, Jonathan walks away like, *Got what I wanted, don't need you anymore.*

I say, "Break. Now what?"

I can still feel it on my arm, where he rubbed it.

Jonathan looks at me. "I think we should have her meet your guy."

"Why would she do that?"

"Because she wants to see what this kid's all about."

"But if she's into building a power base, wouldn't her thing be Evans?"

"Yeah, maybe," says Jonathan sarcastically. "But you won't play her, and it's a little hard to do the split screen in real life."

So, there's my choice: be the governor's wife or get seduced by the governor's wife.

Well, there's no reason Gareth has to fall for her. In fact, maybe it's interesting if he's the only one who knows what she's really all about.

We have her come to the cadet training field. Immediately Jonathan stands a little too close, sort of like he did with me as the governor, but this time much more intense.

He says, "Why is it I hear of nothing but you?"

I refuse to look at him. "I wouldn't know."

Then he reaches out and touches my shoulder. Because I'm not expecting it, I flinch. Then say, "Sorry."

My regular voice comes out, and for a second I'm confused. Did I apologize as Gareth or as me for breaking the game?

Just in time I add, "Ma'am."

Jonathan frowns. "Why are you afraid of me?"

"I'm not."

"Then, why don't you come closer?"

I step closer. Jonathan circles around me once, then again. Making me know I'm not going anywhere. And I feel like I can't. Because Gareth couldn't.

Then he leans in and starts whispering in my ear. I have to stand completely still.

I didn't know before, how much you feel a person when they're close. How you can hear them. Not just what they're saying, but their breathing.

It almost seems like Jonathan's breathing for me.

I hear him. Inside his head. It's like an echo in mine.

I know what he's thinking.

I know he's thinking of doing something, I can feel it.

Part of me thinks it would be okay.

The other part isn't sure.

Is this Jonathan? Or the governor's wife? Or a strange mix of both?

Now he says, "I know what you're thinking. You're wondering if you can leave. But you can't. And that bothers you. Because secretly you think you have power. Even if you pretend to us that you don't. In your mind you're powerful, clever, strong. Only when you step out here with the rest of us mortals, suddenly you discover that in reality you have no power at all. . . ."

His voice has slipped a little. I don't hear the wife's voice anymore.

"I could do anything I wanted. . . ."

Then his hand is on my back. Actually, not my back, but lower.

I jerk away.

"Cut it out." This is me to Jonathan.

He looks at me like I'm nuts. "What?"

"Just . . . stop."

"Stop what?"

"This stupid little game, just cut it out."

"Sorry," he says, "which game? Come on, which game? Because there's only one game I know about, and you're seriously out of character."

He looks genuinely annoyed, but I remind myself: Jonathan is a good actor.

"Who says I'm out of character?"

"I do. You're telling me some guy is going to get all outraged when an attractive female puts a hand on his ass? Give me a break. That's not Gareth, man, that's you."

"Because it was you," I want to say. "And not even really you, but you pretending that we weren't us so you could . . ."

I hate it when you can't say something that makes absolute sense in your head, but you know it will sound ridiculous the second you say it.

He takes a step toward me, flashes his hands in the air. "I mean, what? If I do this, are you going to freak?"

"Stop it," I tell him.

Another step. "Or this? Is this okay?"

I'm not sure what to say: "Yes, because you don't scare me" or "No, because it's not."

"How about this?" He pokes my shoulder.

"No, it's . . ."

"Or this?" This time it's not a poke, it's a shove.

But before he can put his arm down, I throw my arm up. It cracks against his, bone on bone. Hurts, but it feels better than stepping back.

Jonathan moves back, rubs his wrist. He has a weird smile on his face.

"Man, it doesn't take much."

"No, it doesn't."

He looks at me a moment, like he's examining me. I don't know what he sees, and I don't care. I just know I don't like it.

Then he shakes his head. "Yeah, okay . . ."

He grabs his coat off the floor, goes to the door.

I say, "You wouldn't have done it. If I'd really been a guy."

He looks back at me. "Maybe . . ."

Then he yanks the door open. "But news flash, Judith. You're not."

That night I'm sitting on the windowsill with the window open. It's cold, but I don't care. It's almost one in the morning, but I'm nowhere near sleep.

Ever since Jonathan left, this is where I've been. Thinking.

News flash, Judith, you're not.

News flash, Jonathan, I know. I just thought that was okay with you.

The thing about fantasy is you have to agree on what's true. Once someone gets all snotty and says, "That's lame," it's over. Like there are certain people I would never, ever talk to about this stuff because it can sound stupid. Anything you believe in can sound stupid unless the other person gets it.

Which is why I thought it was so cool that Jonathan got it.

But the fact is, you can't trust people with fantasy. It gives them too much power. While you're all happy, thinking, Hey, great, this is how the world should be, they're like, Wham, no, this is how the world really is.

Those people definitely have the edge. They're not as interesting, but when you deal with realities, the rug's not gonna get pulled out from under you.

Like if I fall out of this window, I'm not going to fly. It's just going to be a big mess.

Screw Jonathan.

Screw Evans . . . and Gareth.

Screw the game.

From now on, reality rules.

PART TWO

JUDITH

FIFTEEN

It's strange, being Judith Ellis again.

Judith Ellis says hi to Mrs. Levine in the lobby.

Judith Ellis tries to get Katie to solve the math problem—then gives her the answer when she says she can't.

Judith Ellis doesn't care that there's no e-mail from Jonathan Heitman, because she knows that Jonathan Heitman is a jerk.

And when her dad calls, Judith Ellis is right there to say, "Hi, Dad, how are you? I'm fine."

Actually, when my mom comes to tell me my dad's on the phone, I seriously consider telling her I'll call him back. Because I'm not in the mood.

But then I think of how she'd moan about the phone bill, and I say, "Okay."

As I walk down the hall I try to think what I can tell him. I already told him about Katie. Not really sure I have anything new. That I can tell him about, anyway.

Maybe because I'm thinking about that, I forget to say, "Hey, Dad," when I get on the phone.

After a few seconds I hear, "Judith?"

"Yeah, hi, Dad."

He laughs a little. "Okay, you *are* there. For a second I wasn't sure."

It's weird, I'm feeling a little out-of-body. Almost like I'm watching myself talk on the phone.

My dad says, "How's it—," as I say, "Fine, it's going fine. You?"

"Uh, great," he says. "But tell me what's going on. What are you up to?"

I think. Katie . . . school . . . Mom getting on my nerves . . .

"Nothing."

"Nothing?"

"Yeah, nothing. I mean, same old stuff."

I know I should make it sound like all new stuff. *Hey, Dad, I go to school! I'm taking advanced math! I used to be friends with Leia, but now we hate each other. . . .*

But I just don't feel like it.

The way it's supposed to go is I do all of that and then Dad says, "That's great, honey." But you can't really say "That's great, honey" about "Same old stuff."

Here's what he does say: "Honey?"

"Yeah?"

"Are you okay?"

Which is a completely stupid question, because I haven't said a single thing to make him think things are not okay. I have told him I am fine. I have told him nothing new is happening. I mean, it's not like I got on the phone and said, "Gee, Dad, my life is not a lot of fun right now."

But because I'm not playing the game exactly perfectly, he's all freaked and feeling like something must be wrong.

"Judith?"

"Yeah, Dad, I'm okay." My voice is a little sharp, and I know it isn't going to convince my dad of anything.

So I add, "I'm just kind of tired. School's been a little intense lately."

"Well, sometimes you're a little intense about school. . . ."

Oh, yeah, Dad. You go to Connolly, you see how easy it is to be laid-back and relaxed there.

But I say, "Yeah, I know."

"You still like Connolly, right? Because if you don't, we can talk about that. . . ."

"Connolly's fine," I say.

There's a long pause. Then my dad takes a deep breath. "You know? Right now? I think you should go and do something you really like doing. Okay, hon?"

"Fine." As long as he knows it's his problem, not mine.

"And could you do me a favor?"

"Sure."

"Put your mom on for a moment? There's something I forgot to ask her."

Of course, when I tell my mom Dad wants to talk to her, she gives me a puzzled look, like she expects me to know why. I just shrug. Then I go to my room and shut the door.

Even through the door I can hear my mom yelling.

The next day, on my way to Katie's house, I make a few decisions.

No more TV. No more *Sims*.

No more pretending I'm there to hang out and be friends.

And no more giving Katie the answers.

Katie likes to have the TV on while we work. But today I tell her I can't think while it's on.

She laughs. "I can't think while it's off."

She looks at me like, *Here's where you say, "Oh, okay."*

But I don't. And she turns it off.

We start with the first problem. Katie sort of tries working her way through it. Then she says, "Oh, my God, I have to tell you about this wild thing that happened with *Sims* last night. I figured out a way to burn the entire house down."

"Yeah, okay. But after." I move the math book closer to her.

She sighs and looks at it. "I don't know. My brain feels kind of frozen today."

"Just try."

"Okay, but see, here's where I got to. . . ." She shows me her calculations. She hasn't gotten very far. "And then it all kind of became a blur."

"Well, keep going."

"Can you . . . give me a hint?" She grins, tilts her head.

"Try without it."

She growls, a little, and goes back to the problem.

I hate to admit this, but it feels good to tell Katie no. I think because it's the right thing to do. Frankly, I've been letting her get away with murder.

Then Katie says, "Can we take a break? I'm in serious need of caffeine."

I say, "Sure," and she gets up to go to the kitchen.

"You want anything?" she asks, all hopeful.

"Not really."

She comes back a few minutes later carrying a bag of popcorn and a large bottle of Diet Coke. With a huge sigh, as if she's been working for hours, she settles on the bed, saying, "Okay, where were we?"

I point to the problem.

"Oh, yeah." She munches popcorn. "You know, really. I don't think I'm going to get this without a little help."

I say, "I can't give you more help, Katie."

She stares at me. "You are in a mood. What's up?"

This annoys me. "Nothing, Katie. Just . . . I can't take

the test for you, you know? You're going to have to do this stuff on your own at some point."

"I am doing it," she says.

"No, you're not."

"Well, I'm trying."

"No, you're not."

"It's not my fault I don't get this stuff," she yells. "It's not my fault I'm stupid."

She gets up and goes to her desk. Her hand is at her mouth and she's staring straight at the computer screen.

A second later she starts typing furiously. All over the screen Sims start walking and humming.

I say, "Katie, come on."

"No, it's okay." She points and clicks, points and clicks. "I'm done for today. We can do more next week."

I think of her final. "We're kind of running out of time."

"Yeah, but it's not happening right now. So you can split if you want." She clicks away, and Clarissa starts hurrying down the street.

I say, "Katie." But this time she acts like she doesn't hear me.

And that seriously pisses me off.

I get up from the bed. "Look, will you forget about Clarissa and . . . Hank Hotness for a second?"

Katie laughs. "Hank Hotness? Where'd you get that?"

I hate it that she's laughing at me. Hate it that she can laugh and screw up and flunk out and not care because someone will always be there to save her. That she gets to live in la-la land because she has money, so nothing real will ever, ever touch her.

"This is not life, Katie," I yell. "And you know what? You're never going to have a life, because all you do is float around in some stupid fake world, where you can kill off anyone you don't like, and where you're this skinny, cute chick with a million boyfriends instead of . . ."

The look on Katie's face stops me dead.

I always thought: Everyone is mean to Katie Mitchell. Everyone says she's stupid. Everyone says she's fat.

So you can't be mean to Katie Mitchell. Otherwise you're just a jerk like everyone else.

"I'm sorry" is so useless right now. But I try it anyway.

"I'm being a total jerk, I'm sorry."

For a second it seems like she didn't hear me. Then she whispers, "Yeah, whatever."

I try to say something else, but she just shakes her head.

Then she gets out of the chair and heads to the door.

"I'm just going to . . ." She points down the hall to the bathroom.

I say, "Okay," and think: She's going in there to cry.

"And maybe? When I get back?"

"Yeah?"

"Could you not be here?"

It's only when I'm a block away that I realize I'm headed toward 158 West Seventy-first Street.

For a second I think, Turn around. Go somewhere else, anywhere else.

But I can't. This is the way I go.

I remember when I walked down this street as Gareth. How it felt safer, like a camouflage.

No more Gareth. Judith Ellis now.

I get within a few doors. . . .

And then I run.

My mom isn't home when I get there, and for once I really wish she were, so I could tell her what happened and she could say, "Oh, this isn't nearly as bad as you think it is."

I really need to hear that right now. That it's not as bad as I think it is. That I'm not as bad as I think I am.

I almost never call her at the office. But I pick up the phone and dial her number.

When it rings twice with no answer, I know what's coming.

First the *click*. Then her voice mail: "Hi, this is Nina Ellis. I'm not here right now, but if you'd like to leave a message . . ."

For a second, while the phone's still in my hand, I think of calling my dad.

But it's a totally different time where he is. If I called, he'd be like, "Uh, who? Judith? Oh, yeah, just let me switch over to Dad head. . . ."

Then I think of something else and dial again. While

172

the phone rings, I think, Katie, please pick up, Katie please pick up, please, Katie, pick up. . . .

But all I hear is Katie's mom saying, "You have reached the Mitchell house. To leave a message for Larry, Sonia, or Katie, begin speaking after the tone."

I say, "Uh, hi, Katie, it's Judith. I . . ."

I hesitate. The thing about machines is you can never leave anything real on them. You never know who's going to get the message.

"Call me, or . . . I'll see you at school Monday. Okay, bye."

I really hope she calls me.

I really don't think she will.

I am Judith Ellis, and Judith Ellis is . . .

I can't stand who Judith Ellis is.

And I guess that's why after dinner I go up to the roof.

SIXTEEN

As I go up the stairs I tell myself, No way will he be there.

I tell myself I don't even want him to be there.

But there he is.

He's standing on the third tower. His hands are in his pockets. He looks like the captain of some weird ship.

I stand at the bottom by the ladder.

It's either up or down.

It's not really even that.

I start climbing. As I get near the top I see Jonathan is still standing right by the ledge. For a second it looks like he's not going to let me onto the roof of the tower. Then at the last moment he steps aside, and I pull myself up.

We sit on opposite sides of the ledge. Me with my back to the river, Jonathan facing it. I notice he's sitting as far away from me as possible. I wonder if that's some kind of apology.

Jonathan says, "So, you want to do something?"

"Do you?"

For a while we don't say anything.

Then he reaches down behind the skylight, takes out something in a brown paper bag, and holds it out to me. "Here."

I don't take it right away. It's thick, rectangular. It looks like a book.

"I'm not going to read it," says Jonathan. "So you might as well have it."

I take it out of his hands, feel it under the paper. Definitely a book. With a lot of pages.

I pull the bag off, look at the cover. *The Making of the Atomic Bomb.*

Jonathan says, "Same bomb, right?"

"Yeah."

"I looked for your uncle in the index, but all I knew was Ellis, so . . ."

"Yeah, he has a different last name."

I would never buy this book for myself. It's expensive, I won't understand most of it. . . .

But I love having it. I love holding it, knowing it's mine.

"This is cool. Thanks."

He shrugs. "Welcome."

I guess we could do the game. But I don't really feel like it.

Instead I say, "It's nice up here now. . . ."

"Yeah, not so cold." Jonathan stands up, looks down the stretch of Broadway. It looks like a runway, one big strip, studded with light.

Then he turns toward the park. "You used to be able to see the Natural History Museum from here. Now there's too many buildings."

"I love that museum. I love the blue whale."

"The one they have hanging from the ceiling?" I nod. "When I was kid, I used to think it was real. Like they got a real whale, stuffed it, put it up there."

I laugh. "It would weigh, like, three hundred thousand pounds. Not to mention smell."

"I just thought it was so cool it had to be real."

I want to say we should go there. Right now. Even though the museum's probably closed, I feel like we should go right now and see the whale.

Then Jonathan says, "I got mugged there once. Right outside the park."

"When?"

He shrugs. "I was, like, ten. Guy didn't hurt me, just took my money. But I did think, Okay, screw the museum."

I think about that. It's hard to remember Jonathan at ten. Hard to think of him small enough to get mugged. But I guess everybody is.

Then, without thinking, I say, "That happened to me once."

"What, you got mugged at the museum?"

"No." An image of the blue whale with a gun, saying, "Hand it over." "I mean, um, I got attacked."

He sits down. "On the street?"

"In a doorway. It was night, and I was going to a friend's. The guy followed me off the street."

Jonathan raises his eyebrows. "So, what? Were you okay?"

"Oh, yeah. He didn't . . . do anything permanent." I half smile.

Jonathan waits. I drag my shoe over the tar roof.

"Just, his hands were all over me. Which was kind of gross."

Jonathan makes a face. "What kind of guy?"

"Young. Okay looking. Like he could have been in college. It was weird, I always thought. . . ."

"Yeah, like they'd be some skeevy bum."

"Yeah."

"Big guy?"

"Bigger than me."

Jonathan nods. "So, what happened?"

"This woman who lived in the building came into the lobby. No big deal, she was just going out. But when she saw what was going on, she yelled out, 'Hey,' and the guy split."

"That was lucky."

"Yeah."

"Do you think about what happens if there's no lady?"

"No." It comes out too quick. "No, what I think is, Why'd there have to be a lady? If that makes sense. You know, why did I need someone to . . ."

"Save you." Jonathan just says it.

"Yeah. 'Cause I froze. This guy is there, like, almost on top of me, and his hands are grabbing and . . ." I let out a long breath. "I didn't do anything."

"Come on. Guy was bigger than you. You were, like, how old?"

"Uh, last year . . ." I look out at the river. "I just can't stand it that I didn't do anything. Didn't yell, didn't tell him to stop, didn't kick him, anything. It was like my brain was gone. Like I stopped being."

Jonathan fishes a pack of cigarettes out of his pocket, lights one.

"Where was this?"

"Seventy-first Street. It was night, I was going to see a friend."

"What'd she say? When you told her?"

"I didn't." Jonathan half smiles, half frowns at me. "I mean, what do you do? 'Hi, sorry I'm late, but this guy jumped on me.' I wanted to forget it. So I pretended everything was fine."

I think about it now, what I thought then. How if I told people, everyone I told would remind me of it when I saw them. I'd see it in their faces: *Judithattackedweird*. It'd always be a part of how they saw me.

I remember in seventh grade we had a teacher who got mugged. And whoever it was didn't just take her purse, he really beat her up. She was out of school for months. And when she came back, she had this ugly scar running up the side of her face. From her lip. For a while every time you saw her, that's what you saw first. What you saw second was the fact that she knew that's what you were seeing.

And I didn't want that to happen to me.

158 West Seventy-first Street.

I say, "What's really dumb? I can't walk by where it happened without freaking out. Every time I get near it, my stomach just seizes up and it feels like something awful's going to happen. Like yeah, I got away once, but I'm not going to get that lucky again."

"It's not like the guy's going to come back."

"It's not him. It's the place. The door is like a hole in reality—or what's supposed to be reality. Like the world is supposed to be more or less safe. But when I walk by there, I know it's not. I know what can happen, and how there's nothing you can do about it. I hate that."

"Just a door, man."

I look at him. "Not in my mind."

For a long time we just sit there. Then Jonathan stands up.

"Assignment."

My mom will kill me for being out so late. I know this. She will be worrying, and calling people and freaking.

I could not care less.

I have never been outside with Jonathan Heitman. I mean, away from the building.

I don't even know where we're going. He just walked out of the elevator, through the lobby, and right out onto the street. . . .

And I followed.

Mr. Dalmas was there when we left. I knew he was watching, but I didn't look at him.

I'm not sure Jonathan knows where he's taking us. I know I don't. But I walk like I do. We're walking really fast. Every time you look up, the last street's gone and you're on to the next.

Eighty-fourth Street . . .

Eighty-third Street . . .

The city's really cool at night. I'd forgotten that. Dark night and bright light fighting and merging on the streets. Car horns, subway rumbling, everyone's just . . . going. Going somewhere. Like the whole point is not to get there, but to move.

Like me and Jonathan.

Seventy-seventh Street . . .

Seventy-sixth . . .

I think it is me and Jonathan. Not Gareth and Evans.

And I know where we're going.

When we get to the corner of Seventy-first Street, it's after nine o'clock.

Around when I was supposed to meet Leia that night.

I step back, say, "Okay, fine . . ."

Jonathan says, "Walk."

"No, really, it's cool."

He nods. "Great. It's cool. So walk."

I want to beg: "Don't make me do this."

Because there is always a reason things happen to you. You walk a certain way, and it's the wrong way, or go with the wrong person, and there it is, the bad thing you don't survive. . . .

There is nobody on this street, nobody. The street is deserted, like everybody knows: Stay away.

That's ridiculous, I think. There's moms and kids in bed, and old people watching TV, and people arguing and talking on phones and bored out of their minds and paying bills, there's all kinds of people here. . . .

And they were all there that night, they were all there and it still happened.

So were they really there? Really?

Who was there? You . . . and him.

"Go," says Jonathan.

Then he walks away. Without looking back.

And all that's left is me and the street.

It takes twenty minutes to walk a mile.

A mile is twenty blocks.

So it takes one minute to walk one block.

One minute and I will have done it.

You can die from fear. People do die from it. Their heart goes too fast, and something that was weak to begin with, a vein, a blood vessel in the brain, just goes.

I always wonder if that's what happens when people give up. If they're saying, *I would rather die than deal with this.*

First step . . .

If I run all the way, it'll be over much faster.

But I can't run. That's not the assignment. The assignment is to walk. Normally. As if there is nothing wrong. As if I'm not scared.

The assignment is not to be scared.

Second step . . .

The thing is, you don't make a choice to be scared. Being scared is like being sick. When you're nauseous, and you know you're going to throw up, and it's the last thing you want to do, but you can't help it, you can't stop it. It's there in your guts, and no amount of telling yourself, "You're okay, you'll be okay," will make it go away.

I'm trying to see things as they are, but the shadows are taking over.

Another step. Then another.

I wonder: Is Jonathan watching?

Keep walking. Don't stop.

Third of the way there. Twenty seconds gone.

Forty more to go.

What are the chances that something horrible can happen in the next forty seconds?

I look up at the building numbers. I am at 146; 158 is coming up.

Halfway there . . .

My heart is trying to decide whether to speed up or stop beating altogether. I take a deep breath because I haven't been breathing for a while.

One fifty. Almost there.

I look to the next corner. That's where I have to be. That's where I'm going.

Jonathan is not there.

But he is . . . somewhere. I can feel it.

Or is it someone else? Someone I don't know?

If I look back, it means stopping. And I won't stop.

One fifty-two . . .

I can feel my legs wanting to run. But I won't let them. Run and they run after you. Run and they catch you.

Run and you're afraid.

And I'm not afraid.

Or maybe I am, and it doesn't matter? Because what you say doesn't matter, what you feel doesn't matter.

In the end it's what you do, isn't it?

One fifty-eight . . .

I stop. Right in front of 158 West Seventy-first.

It's just a building. Maybe five stories high. Someone's left Chinese take-out menus on the stoop.

I am still scared. But now I'm mad at the fear, I want to taunt it. This is what you're scared of? Here it is.

The fear fights back, twists my stomach up tight. But being mad helps. It definitely helps.

There are three steps leading to the door. I remember practically running up those steps. . . .

No, no. Don't think about that.

The Chinese take-out menus.

Who leaves take-out menus in a dangerous place?

Every adventure should have a prize of some kind. Something you take from the enemy to prove you're victorious.

I walk up the steps. Take a menu.

Walk down the steps. Then to the next corner.

The light's flashing WALK. But I don't.

Instead I turn around.

And see Jonathan behind me.

SEVENTEEN

"So, is that . . ."

"What?"

Jonathan shakes his head. "Forget it."

It's the first thing he's said since we left Seventy-first Street. We're walking uptown, back toward the building.

Another thing I will do when I work on time travel is to find a way to slow things down. Maybe even stop time altogether. But in a way that you could still think and feel everything in that moment. You'd just get a much longer time to feel it.

On Seventy-seventh Street we pass by a bar, and I say, "Is that Eric's?"

Jonathan looks up. "Yeah."

He slows down, stops a few feet away from the door. "Good old Eric's."

I look, but there isn't much to see. You can't see inside because the door is closed and there are bars on the windows. And behind the bars are neon signs for Bud and Coors. Eric's doesn't look like a place you'd go to have fun. It looks like a place you go when you're really tired.

Jonathan's staring at the door. I know I'm wondering if his dad's inside.

I say, "You want to look?"

He looks up at the Bud sign, shakes his head. "Nah," and we keep walking.

Two blocks later he says, "Usually by now he's home anyway."

For a while I think that's all he's going to say about it. But then when we're waiting at the corner for the light to change, he says, "I know what everybody thinks about him, but he's an okay guy. He doesn't have the greatest temper in the world, but people can be so stupid, if you don't say something, your head explodes."

Then on the next block: "Just sometimes I wish he'd go after the people who are actually screwing him over. Leave me out of it. I mean, what do you say? 'Look, man, I know your life sucks, but I don't take my crap out on you.'"

"What does your mom do?"

"Oh, she gets all into it. Screams at him, but there's no

point. Guy's not even listening. I'm like, Do your thing, call me when it's over."

"Then what do you do?"

"Find someplace else to be."

Time doesn't stop. Eventually we get home.

In the elevator we stand on opposite sides. All of a sudden Jonathan half smiles, and I do too. Like, *Here we are again.*

When we get out of the elevator, he looks at my door. "You going to be okay?"

"Yeah." Primarily because there's nothing my mom could do or say that would mean anything next to this.

"Okay." He nods. For a second it's like he's trying to think of something else to say.

"So—see you."

"See you."

Mom is sitting at the kitchen table when I come in.

From the kitchen you can hear everything in the hallway. So I know she heard.

I say, "Hey. I'm home." Like, *Hi, normal. Not in any chemically altered state.*

"Yeah." She looks up at me in a way that weirds me out.

Then she says, "I don't like this."

"Okay."

"I'm serious, Judith. I do not like this."

"Okay," I say. "I hear you. You do not like this."

Then I go back to my room.

187

■□■□

On Monday morning I'm pretty sure it'll happen again. Once I'm on my own on Seventy-first Street, I'll freak out again.

But even today it really is just a door.

I stand there for a second, looking at it from the street. The eight's crooked. I never noticed that before.

Then a guy comes out with his bicycle, and I keep going down the block.

Now that it's spring, a lot of kids are blowing off the lunchroom entirely. Either they go out, if they're juniors or seniors, or they hang out on the school steps, laughing and yakking. I can totally see why. It's been such a long winter. Sun feels more important than food.

Now all you see in the lunchroom are kids who don't have friends to hang with.

So I have a pretty good idea where I'll find Katie.

Because the cafeteria's practically empty, it's easy to spot her. She's sitting alone at the end of a long table. She's got this stylish little lunchbox, but from the look on her face she's not wild about what's in it. After a second she closes it up and opens a bag of potato chips they sell in the vending machines.

For a second I think, You don't have to do this.

Because I have to admit, I'm nervous. Katie might tell me to drop dead.

She would have a right to. I deserve it.

But that's why I at least have to try.

As I approach her table she's trying to maneuver a chip out of the bag, and at first she doesn't see me.

Then I say, "Hi," and she looks up.

I try, "It's me, the jerk," and she smiles a little.

"Yeah, I thought I recognized you."

Which definitely stings, but I decide to stay put.

After a moment she says, "I'm kidding, you're not a jerk." She holds out the bag. "Want a chip?"

"Sure." I take one. "So, what's up?"

"Um . . ." Katie looks at the ceiling like she's thinking. "My parents are thinking of sending me to boarding school."

"Uck."

"Yeah, I know. Yours truly surrounded by skinny chicks who ski and speak French. Can you say hell on Earth?" She shrugs. "They feel I need a more structured environment."

"Yeah, but what if you pass? And you can stay?"

Katie shrugs. "Guess they don't think there's too much chance of that happening." She looks down at the bag, fiddles with the edge. "Anyway, Connolly without friends pretty much sucks. You need buds if you're going to survive here, you know?"

Sometimes people need a reason to make the effort. . . .

I roll my eyes. "Come on. Kelsey and Jessica?"

"Hey, faux buds is better than no buds."

"No, they're not." I sit down, lean on the table. "Look. I counted it up. It's seven weeks till finals. I was figuring for those seven weeks we could totally buckle down, blitz our way through algebra. Then if the final doesn't work out . . ."

Katie smiles. "You mean if I totally screw up."

"Whatever. But at least you'll know you tried."

Katie thinks. "I guess it can't be worse than skinny chicks who ski."

"Absolutely."

"Or can it?"

For the first week I'm not sure.

I make it a rule that we have to sit in the kitchen until Katie's homework is done. But not only does that mean Katie can't think about anything but math, I can't do anything except watch her think about math. And this, as I find out, can be painful.

Katie's brain does freeze at the sight of numbers. And she's really trying now. So she's trying and freaking and still not getting it.

Like now. She's working on a problem, scribbling away in her notebook. Then she looks at what she's done and starts erasing.

I say, "Let me see," and reach for the notebook.

"No, I made such a stupid mistake. I have to start over."

This time she doesn't even write anything down. Just sits with her head on her hand, frowning at the textbook.

"God," she says softly, "I just don't get this stuff."

"You're stuck," I tell her. "Try another one."

I take her textbook, flip through it for a moment.

"Try this one." I show her.

She looks. "Total Greek."

I roll the pencil toward her. "Just try it."

She picks up the pencil and frowns for a moment, thinking. Then she puts it down.

"Katie, you can do this."

"I can't. Believe me. I'm not lying."

She's not. I know that. But I also know how your brain can trick you, make you see monsters that aren't there.

"Your brain is lying to you. It's telling you you can't do this, but you can because only a stupid person couldn't— and you're not stupid."

She throws up her hands. "How do you know? I mean, some people are, right? Maybe I'm one of those people. I'm part of the Stupid Tribe."

I think. How do I know Katie's not stupid? "Well, for one thing, you're really funny."

Katie shrugs. "You blah-blah as much as I do, occasionally you say something interesting."

"And with *Sims*? You know every last detail of Clarissa's life. You even know how to drown them in swimming pools and burn their houses down."

Katie smiles a little and I push the textbook closer. "Just guess, okay?"

She laughs. "Guess?"

"Yeah, whatever you think the answer is, go ahead and say it."

"But it'll be wrong."

"I don't care. Just say whatever you think."

Katie rolls her eyes. "A billion three million."

"Katie . . ."

"Okay, okay. Uh . . ." She writes a few things down, then looks up, all nervous. "This is going to be so wrong."

"Fine."

"Is it . . ."

She holds up her notebook. I want to jump up and hug her.

"No, but that is so amazingly close."

"Really? I'm in the right universe?"

"You're in the right room. You made one tiny, tiny mistake."

Katie breaks out into a huge grin. "Only one tiny one? Whoa." She reaches out, touches my arm. "Genius is catching."

After that Katie really gets going. Not that she gets all of the answers right. But she gets a lot farther before she makes a mistake than she did before. And when you point it out, she goes, "Oh, yeah, duh. It should be this."

It's funny, when I'm with Katie, I can't be Gareth at all. The two of them do not coexist in any universe. And a lot of the time if I can't be Gareth, I'm kind of bored. But not with Katie. She talks and talks and talks, and for some reason I don't slip back inside my head the way I do in class or with my mom. She's just fun. Like a goofy cartoon movie that you feel a little embarrassed watching, but afterward you think, That was really good. Even though you probably wouldn't admit liking it to anyone who didn't admit it first.

Question: What would Jonathan think of Katie?

Answer: That she was a loser.

Well, then, I guess it's a good thing they don't exist in the same universe.

But now that I think of it, I exist in both their universes. We overlap.

So, what's my universe?

I finally have to go, so Katie walks me to the door. As I wait for the elevator she says, "That was excellent. Really."

"Nah, you were excellent. Told you your brain was lying."

She grins. Then says, "You probably helped Leia all the time, right?"

"With math? Sometimes."

Katie shakes her head. "You know—she is such a jerk. I can't believe her."

"Why?"

Katie opens her mouth. Then she waves her hand. "Nothing."

But it's not nothing. It's just something Katie doesn't want to tell me.

I think of the crumpled piece of paper. Somehow, that note and whatever Katie can't believe about Leia are connected.

"What?"

"Nothing," she says firmly. There's a *ding*. "Hey, see you tomorrow?"

And all I can do is nod and get in the elevator.

And tell myself not to think about it.

I am careful to get home on time these days. Since last week when I stayed out so late with Jonathan, my mom has been monitoring my every move.

Which is why at dinner she asks, "How was the tutoring?" and I know it's a test: *Prove to me you were really at Katie's house. Prove to me you didn't see Jonathan Heitman.*

Part of me wants to tell her something really vague. Like, "Fine," and that's it. Or something she'll know is a lie.

I start to tell her about Katie's big breakthrough. But then the doorbell rings.

My mom says, "Who on Earth is that?"

EIGHTEEN

The doorbell rings again, and I say, "I'll get it."

I look through the peephole, thinking it'll be Mr. Dalmas or Mrs. Chen, who sometimes forgets her keys, so we keep another set for her.

But it's not Mr. Dalmas or Mrs. Chen.

It's Jonathan.

For a second I just stare at him through the glass. Then I open the door.

"Hey."

"Hey." He shrugs slightly. "I guess you guys are having dinner. . . ."

I look back at my mom. "No, I'm pretty much done."

I open the door wide. "You want to come in?"

"Yeah, if it's okay." He steps inside. "Hey, Ms. Ellis."

"Hi, Jonathan." My mom's voice is quiet. She's picking at her food so she doesn't have to look at him.

I gesture down the hall. "You can, uh . . . ," and Jonathan nods, starts walking toward my room.

When I think he can't hear, I say to my mom, "Sorry." Because the whole dinner thing is very important to her.

My mom says, "Yeah."

Like she's sorry too. But I can't tell about what.

Jonathan's sitting on my bed. His elbows are planted on his knees, and his hands are clasped tight. He looks like he's thinking about everything and nothing.

I shut the door. "What's up?"

He shakes his head. "Nothing. Just wanted to be some-place else."

"Oh."

"Sorry about dinner."

"No problem. It was turkey meatloaf night anyway."

He half laughs at that.

Then he says, "Someday it's going to happen."

I don't say anything. But I move away from the door.

"Someday the guy's going to . . ." He looks at his hands like they're showing him the future. "You know, and I don't know what happens then."

I can't decide where to sit. I keep looking at my desk chair, like that's the best place. It feels really far away. But maybe Jonathan wants really far away.

I sit down on the floor at the foot of the bed. I don't know how to ask what I want to ask.

"Is your mom okay?"

"She split, man."

"What do you mean?"

"Said, 'Screw you, I'm outta here.'"

"Whoa."

"Don't get too excited. She'll be back."

He glares at the door like his mom's just come through it. "What she does is go over to her cow friends, and they all suck down the Bud and moan about men. Who's got the lousiest husband? Who's got the worst kid? My mom always wins there. Then when she's tired of that scene, she's like, 'Oh, well, guess it's better than nothing.' Comes home."

"How do you know she moans about you guys?"

"'Cause, man, she used to drag me along with her." His voice goes all high and screechy. "'I'm not leaving you alone with this child. God knows what could happen!' Last few times I've been like, 'You want to go, go. I'm not scared of him.'"

I don't know what to say. Because if I were Mrs. Heitman, I wouldn't leave Jonathan alone with Mr. Heitman.

But now I know being with her isn't so great either.

"What happened? Why'd she leave this time?"

Jonathan drops his head. "My dad got a job."

Confused, I say, "That's good, isn't it?"

"Yeah." He looks up, all fierce. "He's not taking it. And

you know what? He's right not to take it. It's in Atlanta. It pays crap. He told her, 'There are other jobs.' But my mom's all like, 'Yeah, then, why haven't you found any of them?'" He looks away. "That's when he went totally berserk."

For a while neither of us says anything. I lift myself up, sit on the bed a little way away.

Jonathan says, "I actually shouldn't be here. I should go back."

"Why?"

"He could have torn the place apart. You know, or . . ." He shakes his head. "I should just go back."

"I don't think you should."

"No, I can talk him down sometimes."

I don't want to upset Jonathan about his dad any more than he's upset already. But I also really don't want him going back with his dad like that.

"I think you should just stay here."

He looks at me. For a second I think he's going to say, "Screw you. Who cares what you think?"

But he doesn't. "Yeah. Maybe. Until the berserkometer goes down."

Then: "I just hope he doesn't bust up the TV again. That was a real pain in the ass."

I laugh a little, and for a split second it's like that day we had the fight. The day he was so close I could hear him breathe, know what he was thinking.

I guess we're about that close right now.

He leans over, gives my shoulder a little shove with his shoulder.

Then he sits up. "I'm sorry."

"What?"

"No, that was jerky. I forgot."

"It's okay." I give him a goofy grin. "Honestly."

"Yeah, that's okay?"

"Yeah." I put one finger on his hand for a joke. Like, *Tag, you're it.* "That's okay too."

Then: "A lot of things are okay, you know?"

Jonathan says, "Um-hm." Like, yeah, he does know.

The hand I have my finger on loosens up, falls free of the other hand. Now it's my hand it's holding, my fingers weaving in and out of his fingers. Jonathan's fingers are bony, very strong. They get stuck, pull free, get tangled up again.

At first it's like a little game.

Then it's not.

The funny thing about kissing is that in some ways there's not much to it. A mouth on your mouth. In some ways, big deal.

All it is, is a little pressure.

But just like that, everything changes.

All you hear is breathing. And a little bit of heart, from far away.

Does my mom knock first? If she does, I don't hear her.

But all of a sudden there she is. At the door.

Staring.

"I think," she says, "it's time for Jonathan to go."

I say, "Ma," but Jonathan's already up.

I tell him, "Wait," but he just waves his hand like, *We're not doing this.*

And I'm like, *What? What are we not doing?*

So Jonathan leaves. But my mom stays right by my door. Waiting for the big Explanation.

Really she doesn't want an explanation. She already thinks she knows what she saw.

Which is, frankly, a lot more than I know right now, and until I decide what this is, I don't want to say a thing about it. Especially not to her.

So I tell her, "I don't want to talk about it."

"Oh, I'm sure you don't."

God, I hate the way she sounds. So superior, so . . .

I tell her, "You don't know what this is. You seriously do not."

"Then, please explain."

"No." Because there is no point in explaining to someone who's already made up her mind.

"Well, then, explain to me if you've been lying to me all this time. Because I specifically remember the words 'just friends' coming out of your mouth."

"We are friends."

She gives me a look.

"We are."

"Honey, come on. . . ."

I want to scream. Scream until she stops talking, scream so she never talks again. I hate every word that comes out of her mouth.

This is mine, I want to tell her. *Maybe I don't know what it is, but you don't get to tell me, because this is mine. My life, and I get to decide.*

She takes a deep breath. "Baby, I know you think you can handle this, and that I should just butt out. . . ."

"Correct."

"But I can see—"

"What?" I yell. "What do you see?"

My mom's a little surprised, but she stammers, "Things that . . . that maybe you can't right now."

"Like what, Mom? Why do you think I'm so helpless?"

My mom looks shocked. "I do not think that you are helpless—"

"Oh, yeah? Then, why do you act like I can't handle anything? Like there's this danger, and that terror and bogeymen are everywhere, and I'm just going to . . ." I can't even imagine it, what my mother thinks. "Be destroyed."

My mom waits a moment before answering. She's afraid of this conversation, I can tell. Good, I'm glad she's afraid.

In a different voice she says, "Honey, I know you're a very strong kid."

"No, you don't."

"I do."

"No, you don't." I lean against the edge of my desk, because I'm calm right now and I want to show her that. "You don't say it like that if you really think it. You sound like a shrink or something. How do you feel?"

"I . . . worry." She takes a deep breath, but this time I wait. "I worry that there are a lot of . . . I don't know what you want to call them, dangers, creeps, whatever, in the world and yes, I do worry about you. That's kind of my job."

She smiles. Like, *We're friends now, right?*

"What do you think is going to happen to me?" My voice is very hard and steady.

"Um, pick a nightmare, you know?" She throws up her hands, laughs a little. "But okay, maybe too much. I hear you. 'Back off.'"

"What do you think? I mean it, I want to know."

"I think backing off means I don't give you a list of my worst-case scenarios."

So I think of her worst-case scenarios. I think of Jonathan, and what she thinks of him, and of me for being with him, and how to her that's the most vile thing, the thing she really has to worry about. . . .

I take a deep breath. "The thing is, if you're worried that I'm going to be attacked by some lunatic? That's already happened. Okay? It happened, and it's over, and you can cross it off your list. You can stop worrying."

My mom stares.

"So, okay?" Suddenly it's like someone took all my

vocal cords and twisted them tight. But I keep talking, partly because I don't want to hear what my mom will say next. "We can stop thinking about it. 'Cause it happened and I'm fine, and people can be okay when these things happen. You know? There are worse things."

Really quietly my mom asks, "When did this happen?"

I hate giving it a time. That makes it real. "Last year."

"When last year?"

"Like, spring, summer. But the thing is, it doesn't matter."

My mother comes up to me. "What are you saying? Of course it matters." She takes my hands, grips them real hard.

Up till now I always thought, Don't, don't say anything, and now I know why. Because I don't feel anything about this now, and she's all freaked. And she is not going to accept that I'm okay about it, I know that. She's going to demand that I be this complete and utter wreck.

My mom is saying something to me, but I haven't really clued in. ". . . what happened, just tell me. . . ."

So I do.

What's funny about that night is that it was raining. So I was wearing a raincoat. From behind all this guy probably saw was a yellow blob.

And you kind of wonder—at least, I do—what was it that made him think, Oh, yeah, I want to . . . whatever . . . that?

Miss Hot I was not, that's all I'm saying. And I know

they say that doesn't matter, it doesn't matter how you're dressed or if you look sexy, it's not about that at all. I do know that, but still, it's weird to find out it's actually true. That they don't just say it to make you feel better.

You didn't do anything to make it happen.

Which sometimes sounds like, *And you couldn't do anything to stop it either.*

You basically have no control.

Part of me would rather think I did do something wrong. That it was all about something I did and that if I change that one thing, it won't ever happen again.

But how I dressed wasn't it. And where I was wasn't it, either. It wasn't like I was on some dangerous street. I only walk it every day on my way to school.

I didn't even yell. That woman came out of her apartment just because . . . I don't know. She was going somewhere or getting dog food.

Every once in a while I think, Okay, what if the dog hadn't run out of food?

After I tell my mom the whole thing, I take the longest hot bath I have ever taken. Like, I feel poached when I get out. And really, really tired.

It seems unbelievable that all this happened today.

When I get out, she has my duck robe ready, the one I always wear when I'm sick. I smile a little and put it on.

But I tell her, "I'm okay. Seriously."

She smiles, rubs my back. "I know you are. I know that."

"Like . . . don't call in the shrink brigade or anything."

"Okay. No shrink brigade."

"And don't freak out about Jonathan."

She smiles, keeps rubbing my back.

"Okay?"

The smile goes. "Jonathan . . ." Then it comes back. "We don't have to talk about Jonathan right now. I'll . . ."

I wait. But all my mom says is, "Why don't you get some sleep?"

Later that night I get out of bed and turn on the computer. I get into e-mail, type in, **Irgan@connect.com.**

> **Jonathan,**
> **Hope the TV is okay.**
> **Jude**

The next morning, I get up really early, before my mom's awake or anything. It's just starting to be light out.

I open e-mail and read:

> **Jude**
> **TV's okay.**
> **A lot of things are.**
> **Someone said that so I guess it's true.**
> **Jonathan**

NINETEEN

But then, that's it.

No more messages.

For a week.

Then longer . . .

At first I think something happened.

Something worse than the TV.

Then I think, No.

I tell myself that if something truly bad had happened, I would know about it. I would have seen police or heard people in the building talking about it.

I even think my mom would tell me. If something had happened to Jonathan.

So he's probably okay.

So, good.

Only, where is he?

A few days later I'm running out of the lobby, headed for school, when I see a taxi pull up in front of the building. After a second I see Mrs. Heitman get out.

I can't tell: Is she *back* back? Or just getting her stuff?

She looks really tired, even though it's only eight in the morning. When she sees me, she smiles a little and says, "Hi there, hon. How are you?" in a hoarse voice, just like Jonathan's.

"Fine," I say. "How are you?"

"Oh, you know." She laughs. "Been better."

And she disappears into the building.

I don't want to discuss Jonathan with my mom. But that night I can't help saying, "Mrs. Heitman's back."

My mom nods over the dishes she's washing.

"You knew she left?" I ask.

"Um-hm." My mom keeps her eyes on the dishes.

"Do you think she's going to stay?"

My mom sticks the sponge inside a coffee mug, starts scrubbing hard. "Oh, I expect she will."

I want to ask why my mom thinks that. What she knows about it all.

And if what she knows changes what she thinks about Jonathan. Because how can it not?

But before I can ask any of this, she takes a bunch of plates out of the drying rack and hands them to me. "Could you put these away, please?"

And I know she's not going to talk any more about it.

Later, in my room, I sit at my computer.

First I write:

Hey, Jonathan,
I saw your mom. Is it okay having her back?

Then start again.

I saw your mom. Is she back? When my parents split, my dad came around a few times to get his things, and I always thought, Oh, he's back now. But obviously he wasn't. So I know

Then I stop. Because the fact is, I don't know anything. Because Jonathan hasn't told me anything.

Which could mean it's something too awful to tell or else . . .

Or else . . .

I can't believe Jonathan Heitman would get freaked out over a kiss.

Or kissing. I guess you'd have to call it kissing.

I mean, tongues, right. So . . .

Whatever. I can't believe it'd be that big a deal to him.

To me, a mouth touching my mouth is a big deal. A kiss where you taste someone, feel them liking it, feel yourself lose it a little . . .

I still can't quite believe that was me.

So, in a way, it doesn't have to be me. Doesn't have to be us.

To Jonathan I'm sure it's total bush league. Something he did in second grade in a dopey spin-the-bottle game.

I'm sure he's not a virgin. Whereas I am, in just about everything.

Maybe he didn't like it. That's a very reasonable explanation for his disappearance. That would be pretty awkward. *Hm, maybe it was a big thing for you, but for me? Well, it was more exciting than watching the toilet flush—and that's the best I can say for it.*

I look at his last message. The first time I read it, I thought it meant all this stuff. Now I don't know. Because Jonathan was also, like, I'm not doing this. And I never did find out what "this" was. I guess . . . not what I thought.

So, what he has to know is that it wasn't a big thing.

Hey, Jonathan,
If you think what happened is weird, don't
worry. No big deal.

I look at that message for a while. Try to see what it really says.

One thing I learned with Leia: Don't push. No matter how casual you try to sound, people know. And it makes them nervous. Annoys them.

Stay cool.

Don't say anything.

I hit Delete.

"Helloo, where are you?"

Katie waves a hand in front of my face. "Earth to Judith, come in Judith. . . ."

I sit up. "God, sorry."

Katie laughs. "No problem. Nice to know someone else spaces from time to time. What were your deep thoughts?"

That it's been almost three weeks and I still don't know what's going on with Jonathan.

I shake my head. "Nothing."

My mom says Katie is lucky she has me for a tutor. I think she's wrong. Right now I'm lucky to be Katie's tutor. Because that's the only thing that stops me from thinking about Jonathan and why he isn't around.

Katie is doing a lot better. But she still makes mistakes, and when she makes too many of them, she gets down on herself and gives up. Exactly what can't happen in the final.

Like now. A few minutes ago she screwed up something really simple, and I can tell she's starting to freak.

She pulls at her hair. "This is what's going to happen on the test, I'm going to go totally blank."

"No," I tell her, "it won't. You are going to be so

obnoxiously prepared you're going to be the first one to finish."

"Yeah." She grins. "Because I'll have written 'clueless' for all the answers."

A few minutes later the phone rings and Katie goes to answer it.

It's always weird when you're right there and someone's talking on the phone. They know you can hear, but you have to pretend not to. While I flip through one of Katie's magazines, I hear her say, "Oh, hey, Mom. Really? Whoa, biggie, biggie. What are you going to wear? Yeah, there's stuff in the fridge. No problem."

She sighs. "No, I will not. Yes, I promise." She rolls her eyes at me. "Anyway, Judith's here, and . . . Judith. The girl who's helping me with math. The brilliant one." She grins at me. "Okay, so anyway, get his autograph, okay? See you tomorrow."

She hangs up. "*Mes* parents are out. How do you feel about ordering a pizza?"

I think about going home. Another dinner with my mom watching me for signs of Jonathan contact, me wishing there were signs of Jonathan contact . . .

More silence on the e-mail. More silence, period.

I say, "I feel really excellent about pizza, as a matter of fact."

"Your mom and dad go out a lot." I pull a slice of pizza out of the box, slide it onto a plate.

"Yeah, thank God." I look at Katie, trying to see if she

means it. "No, seriously. Dinner with them is a torment. They're both skinny skinny, and it's like, who's the elephant at the table?"

"They don't say that."

"Not in actual words, but . . ." Katie chews and swallows. "Last year my mom put me on this diet. Then Kelsey and Jessica became total turd women, and it was like, Eat everything! You wouldn't believe how much I ate waiting for those chicks to call." She mimes. "Look at phone. Eat cookie. Look at phone. Eat cookie."

I laugh. "With me and Leia, I was the one who did all the calling."

"Yeah, I know."

I look at her. "What do you mean?"

Katie looks flustered. "No, well . . . just what you said." She picks up her slice, takes a bite.

"But you said, 'I know.' How could you know? I never said anything about it."

Katie sighs, turns the plate around so the crust is facing her.

Then she says quietly, "Look, I told you Leia was a jerk."

She did. She did tell me that.

Now I know why.

I can't believe she told people.

Can't believe she wouldn't talk to me, but then she goes and tells everyone else . . .

What?

My stomach is tight, like before a big test that I know I'm not ready for. It's dumb, we're just talking about words, what people say. But it feels much, much more real than that.

I say, "What is she telling people about me?"

Katie doesn't say anything.

"That I called her a lot, right?"

Katie nods. "Yeah, basically."

I look down at my lap. "Well, I wouldn't have if she'd only . . ." I take a huge, deep breath. "If she hadn't disappeared on me, you know?"

"I totally know," says Katie. "Believe me, I know."

"It's like one day someone's your best friend, the person you count on to . . . and the next they're gone, and they don't even feel like they have to explain it? Like you're not supposed to care? 'Sorry, that wasn't real. That didn't happen.'"

I know I'm sounding out of control now. And suddenly it feels like I'm not even talking about Leia, but about this huge other thing that Leia's only a part of.

But if I think of what that other thing is, I'll lose it entirely.

Katie hands me a piece of paper towel. "Here. You want to freak, go ahead."

I blow. "No, that's okay."

"Really. I do it all the time."

I can't help it. I laugh a little. The image of Katie freaking is funny somehow.

213

I sniff, feel like I can say it if it's a joke. "So, what? Does Leia say I was, like, in love with her or something?"

Katie rolls her eyes. "Who cares?"

I ball up the paper towel, leave it on the table. "What do you mean?"

"I mean, who cares what Leia says? Who cares what Leia thinks? Maybe she's right, maybe she's wrong—*I* don't know. But if she's got this huge problem with it, screw her.

"It's like the fat thing," she says. "K&J were always, like, 'You're fat, you're this tacky, stupid, unworthy thing.' And I was, like, 'Gosh, I am fat—I must be this tacky, stupid, unworthy thing.' But you know, once we weren't friends anymore, I looked at them, and I was, like, 'Okay. I am fat. But my clothing sense is *way* better than yours. Plus, I think I have just a *few* more brain cells.'"

I sniff/laugh. "Just like a billion."

Katie fiddles with her pizza crust like she's trying to figure out whether to eat it or not. "Why let Leia decide what it all means, you know? What do *you* think?"

I realize: I don't know what I think. And that's why I want to know what Leia thinks.

And Katie's right. That's screwed up.

Katie smiles. "I think it's cool you called her. Make her confront you, that's what I say."

She makes a fierce face, like she's about to punch someone out, and I laugh.

Katie would be a good superhero.

Later, when I'm getting ready to go, I say, "How's Clarissa?"

Katie makes a face. "Ugh. Drama, drama, drama."

"Yeah, how so?"

"Well, Nick Nice Guy, remember? He asked her out." I nod. "But I'm not so sure I should let her say yes. I mean, she's a goddess, he's a loser."

"So make her say no."

"Well, I thought about it, but then I thought maybe I'm being really shallow. Maybe because he's a nerdly nerd, he'll see things in her other boys don't. You know, all the other guys, it's like, 'Whoa, hot mama in a miniskirt.' Nick doesn't rate that high on the hotness meter, so she wouldn't have to worry so much about how she looks. Which would be good, but he is this total geek."

I have to roll my eyes at that one. "So why don't they hang? I mean, why do they have to do the whole boyfriend/girlfriend thing?"

Katie looks outraged. "Hey—this could be true love! Unfettered by superficial assumptions."

"Oh, sorry."

Katie thinks about it. "I don't know. Maybe I'll just electrocute him."

On the way home I think if there is such a thing as true love, it probably doesn't involve hotness meters or miniskirts or who calls who.

If it does, forget it.

Why can't people just be? Why does there always have to be this stupid "Ooh, you like them" crap? I mean, first Leia . . .

I like you.

No, you like me too much.

But what's too much? When does it become this weird, bad thing?

That's what I'm thinking about when I walk into the lobby.

So hard that I don't see Jonathan until he's almost right in front of me.

Okay, he's here and I'm here. This is not pushing. This is just . . . what is.

Too loud, I say, "Hey."

It sounds horrible, echoing all over the lobby.

He stops, turns. Doesn't look too surprised to see me. Doesn't look too thrilled to see me either.

He says, "Hey."

And it's exactly how he would have said it a year ago, when we didn't know each other at all. Not mad, not nasty. Just . . . bored.

And of course I don't have a clue what to say.

It can't be nothing. Can't be, "How are you? I'm fine."

For forever those stupid "Hey's" float between us, waiting for someone to grab on.

Just when I'm about to say, "You know, this is dumb . . . ," Jonathan says, "Yeah," and it's not my turn anymore. "Sorry, I gotta be somewhere. I'm late."

"Oh."

A smile that's not a smile. "I'll see you around."

"See you around" is what people say when they won't see you at all. I know this.

So I smile like it's all good, all casual, and say, "Sure."

Because maybe the best thing to do when someone thinks you like them too much is to act like you don't like them at all.

That way, you're not guilty.

In the elevator I think of all these things I wanted to ask him. Like if his mom is staying.

If his dad is hanging out at Eric's. If he's stopped going berserk.

Basically, what I want to know is if he's okay.

And because of that stupid, ridiculous kiss . . .

I can't.

Which just makes no sense at all.

TWENTY

As I walk through the door my mom calls out, "Hey, just in time!"

I take a second to make sure my face is normal, that it shows no sign of what just happened. Then I go into the kitchen, where my mom's stirring this big pot of sauce. The kitchen smells all garlicky.

She says, "I had this intense craving for spaghetti. What do you think?"

I try to smile. "I think cool." My stomach is all tight, and I don't actually feel like eating. But my mom knows the spaghetti she makes is one of my favorite meals.

Which is a very small nice thing.

And right now, with everything else sucking out loud, that's a very good thing.

We should probably let the sauce cook longer, but my mom says she's starving, so we decide to eat now. She spills everything into a huge bowl and brings it to the table with a big *Ta-da!* I air-applaud, cry, "Bravo, bravo."

I hold out my plate while my mom puts spaghetti onto it. "It looks really good," I tell her.

"Well, we'll see."

Mom asks me all about Katie, and I tell her how I think she may pass her final. "Which would be cool, because then they'll let her stay at Connolly."

My mom smiles. "You'd miss her if she left?"

"Yeah. She's cool."

"That's nice. I'm glad." She puts some salad into my bowl. "How're you feeling about everything else?"

I look at her. "Everything else" could be Jonathan, which I don't want to talk about with her.

Or it could be the attack, which she's been pretty cool about. Because she's been nice and made me spaghetti, I decide that's what it is.

"I'm . . . okay. You know, I had almost a whole year to freak out about it."

She winces, and I know she's thinking about all that time she didn't know.

I say quickly, "But I think I'm sick of being scared. If that makes any sense."

"Makes a lot of sense." She forks up some spaghetti.

"But I think you should also realize that something did happen to you, and that you might be feeling a little shaky right now."

I want to say: "I was. I was definitely feeling not okay with the world. But actually, Mom, the person who made me feel a lot better is . . ."

Just as I'm thinking how to tell my mom about Jonathan getting me to walk past the door at night, she says abruptly, "You should know something. I had a talk with Mrs. Heitman."

I go cold. I can't believe this. I cannot believe this.

"And I think it went well," my mom adds, watching me.

I slide my fork into my spaghetti. I'd like to go on eating—it's the only other thing to do at this table right now—but I can't.

No wonder Jonathan hasn't said anything. No wonder he . . .

I can't believe how much damage they do, and all the time, they think they're so right.

I know my mom wants me to ask what they talked about, but I'm not going to. I refuse to take this seriously.

Very quietly I say, "Fine."

My mom waits for a moment, but I'm done, so she says, "Fine what?"

"You talked to Mrs. Heitman. That's fine."

"I don't know. . . ."

"Because nothing is going to be different. And you

wanted to talk to her, so you did, and fine." I look at her. "But nothing is changing."

"I wouldn't be entirely sure about that, honey." Now my mother's voice is all soft. She's acting like she's sorry, but I know she's thrilled.

I want to scream at her: "How can you act like you know things when you don't? How can you just decide what everything is when you haven't got a clue? Why do you think you absolutely know what everything means?"

What I should do, right now, is get up and go across the hall to Jonathan's apartment.

But that would be different. And I said nothing would be different.

And nothing will be. Nothing is changing.

No matter what my mom and Mrs. Heitman talked about.

I look down at the spaghetti. Now that I know what it's for—*Look, honey, I made your favorite, don't be mad*—I can't eat it.

It's a general rule I have with my mom: Don't show her you're angry. Once she knows you're angry, it's her way in. She gets to talk to you, to treat you like you're some warped, damaged piece of goods.

But I think this time I'm so angry she may not be able to do that.

I put down my fork. "I'm actually not hungry."

She makes a sad face. Like something bad happened to me that she had nothing to do with.

She reaches for my hand, but I take it off the table.

"You don't have power over this," I tell her. "You do not get to decide."

And to make her understand that, I get up from the table and go to my room.

So now I know. Why Jonathan was so weird.

Why he acted like he was both annoyed with me and scared of me.

He must think I'm an idiot. How pathetic, to have my mommy tell his mommy, "Hey, keep your kid away from my little girl."

I should e-mail him. Tell him I knew nothing about this.

But what should I say? "Hi, sorry my mom's a jerk."

I feel guilty, like it's my fault. Like I asked my mother to do this, even though I didn't. Parents have that power, to control how people see you, what they think of you. She opens her big, stupid mouth, and all of a sudden we're back to Jude the Prude and Jonathan the Head Case.

But if I'm totally honest, I know this isn't just about my mom.

It's also the other thing.

I don't know. Maybe it is better to leave it alone for a while. That's obviously what Jonathan wants.

Don't push. Say nothing.

But I'm sick of it. The pretending everything is no big deal. Pretending you don't care.

Then, for some weird reason, I remember what Jonathan said about Terryn. How he hated that he was always sneaking around, pretending he wasn't there.

How he needed to be drawn into honest combat.

So. Okay.

Honest combat it is.

I've never been to Jonathan Heitman's house. Even when we were kids and people had birthday parties, I never went to his. And he never came to mine. I mean—him coming over to my house that first time was a big deal. But somehow his house was always totally off-limits.

Well, now I'm going to have to.

I have to think of it like an assignment. A risk you have to take to prove yourself.

The next afternoon when I come home, I wait until four thirty. Then I open my front door and go out in the hallway.

As I step up to the Heitmans' door I remind myself there's no guarantee Jonathan's going to be home. . . .

But I have to do this, have to do something daring, break the rules somehow.

Of course I can't do it right away. Of course I stand there like an idiot, staring at the bell for what seems like forever.

Did I plan what I was going to say? If I did, I've forgotten.

Just ring already.

I poke the little white circle. But not hard enough, and nothing happens.

This time I use my thumb. And really press. The bell sounds loud, like an alarm. I whip my hand away, like, *Wasn't me.*

And wait.

It's like that dumb old game you used to play. Ring somebody's bell, then run for the stairs. *"Who's there?"* Hee, hee, hee . . .

Actually, I bet Jonathan did a lot of that.

What am I doing here? Obviously no one's home.

Count to three, then turn around and go back to your own house.

One . . .

I hear someone moving around. Oh, God, someone really is there.

Two . . .

Footsteps now, coming toward the door. Take a deep breath.

The latch on the peephole slides up. A shadow behind it. I can't see who it is, but they can see me.

My heart is pounding. My hands are all numb.

The door cracks open. In my mind I've been thinking, Jonathan, so the first thing I think when I see Mr. Heitman is, Old.

And, Just got out of bed.

Because that's what he looks like. His hair's all ragged, and his clothes are rumpled and stale. Exactly like he slept in them.

This is not a man who wants to be seen. Not like this.

He swallows hard, tries to straighten up. "Yeah."

His voice is quiet. But there's something strange and tense in it. He's holding the door only a little way open.

As softly as I can, I say, "Hi, Mr. Heitman. I'm, um, Judith Ellis, from next door?"

He nods, keeping his eyes on me. For a weird split second I think, He's scared of me.

But that's insane. Mr. Heitman's, like, a foot taller than me. And heavy. His hands on the door are big and red, with thick, fleshy fingers.

"I was wondering if Jonathan was home."

He frowns, like he didn't hear me.

So I try again, "Um, is Jonathan—"

But Mr. Heitman interrupts. "No, he's not here. Why?"

"No reason." I'm whispering now. "I just wanted . . ."

Whatever it is I want, Mr. Heitman doesn't want to hear it. He takes one unsteady step forward, and immediately I step back. And shut up.

He says, "Now, look. Your mother came by, she said what she wanted to say. Fine. Jonathan's doing what she asked. So, you do us all a favor and do the same."

He points right at me. "Jonathan's not going to bother you, and you're not going to bother him, and that way everybody's happy. Right?"

I'm scrambling for a way to say, "No, that's my mom, it's not me," when all of a sudden Mr. Heitman shouts, "Right?"

And I know absolutely that if I say anything other than

"Right," this man will not be in control anymore, and that is not something I want to see.

So I say, "Right."

But by that time the door's already closed.

So one thing's clear: I'm not going to see Jonathan at home.

Actually, anywhere with parents is out of the question.

I try to remember: What did Irgan do to catch Terryn?

Got him alone where no one was watching.

So that's what I have to do.

Where is Jonathan? Where does he go?

The roof . . . and the basement.

Jonathan's out there somewhere moving around. So if I keep moving around, it stands to reason we'll end up in the same place at the same time.

TWENTY-ONE

For a week I take the garbage down to the basement every night.

Only, Jonathan isn't down there.

After school I go up to the roof.

But he's not there, either.

And he's never in the lobby. Or in the hallway. Or in the elevator.

So, how do you reach someone when you don't even know where they are?

I look at my computer. It's weird how even if you have no idea where someone is, you can always reach them online. It's a place where nobody actually exists, but there's a particle, a dust mote, of everybody in the world.

So. E-mail. Only one problem.

I have no idea what to say.

And until I do, I have to just shut up. Because this e-mail is too important to screw up.

Ms. Isaacs has started giving Katie practice tests. We did the first one together. I didn't give her any answers, but I did help her out when she got stuck.

Today she got the second test. I'm getting the soda out of the fridge when all of sudden she says, "I think I should do this on my own."

"Okay." I set the soda down on the kitchen counter.

"I mean, like you shouldn't even be here." She looks up at me. "Because if you are, I'm going to ask for help, and I have to stop doing that."

I say, "You're sure?" Because I'm a little worried that Katie's not ready for this.

"Well, no. But I'm the one who has to take the test, right?"

I nod. "True."

"So . . . get out of here."

So I do.

Everyone's thinking finals now—finals and summer. Everyone's crazy stressed out and cramming like mad. But at the same time all you want to do is run out to the park and lie in the sun.

Any day when the weather's nice, people go nuts. Like today. It's warm, breezy. No one wants to be inside. Especially in Mr. Jarman's class, because it's the last one of the day. As we all walk in Michael Ruddick says, "Permission to blow off class, sir. Due to fabulously clement weather."

I look over at Mr. Jarman, thinking he'll laugh. But instead he says, "Sit down, Michael," in this voice that lets you know you better sit down—and fast.

Within five seconds it becomes obvious: Everyone else may have spring fever, but Mr. Jarman is in a seriously rotten mood.

It does happen. Teachers get pissy. Something goes wrong at home, their kid's sick or whatever. They don't want to be here any more than you do, and they let you know it.

Usually when teachers pull the "Hey, I'm a person too" routine, I think, Well, you're getting paid to be here, I'm not. But I can't think that with Jarman because he's so cool most of the time.

He is definitely not cool today. He's firing off question after question, really fast and aggressive. He goes so fast, people get confused. And when they screw up, he corrects them in this tired, sarcastic voice, like they're the biggest morons on Earth.

After a while people just stop raising their hands.

Jarman snaps his fingers. "Come on, people, let's go. Wake up. Anybody here but me?"

No answer. He taps on the board with his knuckles.

I'm not the only one who jumps. People glance at one another like, *What is his deal?*

Jarman asks another question. But this time we give him the silent treatment. You want us to talk? Screw you.

Which is sort of not cool. I mean, yeah, Jarman's in a crummy mood, but he's not a crummy guy. I look around the table. Michael, Madelyn, even David the suck-up—they've all got blank faces on, like, *Did you hear someone say something? Nope, I didn't hear anybody.*

I think, Come on, guys. Don't be jerks.

Jarman's looking around the table; he sees it too. This is the first time the class has ever turned on him—which sucks, because he doesn't deserve it.

Quietly he repeats the question.

No answer.

"Is there anybody out there?" wonders Jarman. "Do I see dead people?"

Normally we'd laugh, but not this time. Nobody's giving an inch.

I hate this. It's torture. It feels like we're letting him down.

Jarman throws his hands up, lets them fall. "Anybody?"

That's when I raise my hand.

Basically because I can't stand the silence anymore.

Mr. Jarman points. "Ms. Ellis," he says.

And that's when I realize: I don't have the slightest clue what the answer is.

I hear myself say, "Oh, my God," and burst out laughing.

Actually, everybody does. Even Mr. Jarman.

■□■□

After class I'm on my way out the door when Jarman says, "Ms. Ellis."

I turn around. Jarman is gathering up papers on the desk, putting them into his briefcase.

He says, "I hear from Ms. Isaacs that Katie Mitchell's making good progress."

"That's great. Does she . . ." I'm not sure I can ask this, but why not? "Does she think Katie's going to pass?"

"Well, ultimately it's up to Katie, but Ms. Isaacs feels reasonably optimistic. So, congratulations." He smiles. "How'd it feel?" He nods at the chair where I was sitting, and I know he's talking about my mistake.

I laugh. "I hope I never screw up like that again."

"That wasn't a screwup. Everyone sitting here silent and pissed off—that was screwed up."

I smile. Mr. Jarman smiles back.

"I hope to see you next year, Ms. Ellis."

"Maybe next year I'll get the answer right."

"You think if you have the answer right, you won't be scared."

This seems so obvious I have to think about it. "Yeah, because then you're sure."

"Life is too short to wait till you're sure, Ms. Ellis. Good luck with your finals."

When I get home, I go to the computer.

I still don't know what to write. But that doesn't seem to matter so much anymore.

231

To: Irgan@connect.com
Subject: Assignment
**Tomorrow night. The 13th floor. Third
tower. 2000.**

But that's not enough. I need something more.

I think. All the obvious stuff. "I really hope you come.
I want to talk to you." None of it sounds real.

Then I think of it. And type . . .

Scared?

The next night at seven thirty I tell my mom I'm going out.

She looks at me. Every part of her wants to say, "You
stay right here."

But she can't. It's funny when you realize it. They actually don't have all the power.

All she says is, "I'll be here."

And Jonathan might not be.

I mean, he might not show at all.

That's one of the things I think about, waiting on the
roof.

I sit on the ledge of the tower, catch the wind coming
off the river. The water looks silver gray at night, like the
sky lying on the earth. It makes you think about where it
might take you. Cars zoom up and down the West Side
Highway. You're in the middle of everything, but you can
still *be*. The world feels like it belongs to you. To everybody,
but also to you.

If Jonathan doesn't come . . .

Then, he doesn't come.

And that's it. He's just another person that isn't any-more. Like Leia and kind of like my dad.

But that actually isn't true. Because even if he isn't, he absolutely was.

I mean, I think about what I was like when I thought he was just Jonathan the Head Case.

Definitely another person that isn't anymore—and that's a good thing.

I start thinking about people who weren't then but are now, people like Katie, when I hear the roof door creak as it swings open.

I turn, look over my shoulder. Watch Jonathan walk toward me. At the bottom of the ladder he stops, looks up.

He says, "You've got to stop."

And I say, "Why?"

For a long moment he stares at me. Then he starts climbing up the ladder.

When he reaches the top, he says, "Ask your mom."

"Yeah, I know. I'm sorry. I didn't know she'd said any-thing when I saw you in the lobby."

He's looking for a place to sit down. I watch where he chooses.

Opposite ledge. Facing me.

"I guess she thinks she's protecting you." He turns, glances at New Jersey. When he turns back, he says, "And maybe that's not totally crazy."

There's something about this I don't like. My mom and Jonathan agreeing, for one thing. This idea that I have to be protected. It feels like a cheap excuse.

"Why? What are you going to do to me, Irgan?"

He looks at me like he can't figure me out right now. He starts to say one thing, then stops.

I say, "What?"

"No, nothing." He's annoyed now, doesn't like being pushed.

"Just say it."

"There's nothing to say. Look, I don't need to screw anyone else up."

"So don't."

He sighs. Like everything should be so simple.

But everything is that simple, really.

He starts grinding the heel of his boot into the roof. It makes a gritty, uncomfortable sound. "Things got a little intense, okay? I was freaking out over my dad, and it was . . ." He looks at me, decides he doesn't want to say what it was.

What he does say is, "The thing is, I don't need a girl-friend right now."

"I don't want to be your girlfriend."

He frowns. "What? You think we're just going to keep playing the game?"

"No. I don't know. I think this is different."

"Oh, yeah." He laughs. "This is different."

He stands up, folds his arms. He says quietly, "I don't know what this is."

He glances over at me. Then he sits back down.

But next to me.

For a while neither of us says anything. Then I say, "How was the TV?"

He laughs. "It was okay. Other things suck, but the TV was okay."

"Your mom's back."

"Yeah. For now. You want to know why she came back?"

"Why?"

"Because my dad took the job."

"Oh. The one—"

"In Atlanta, yeah."

"Wow, that's . . ."

I don't want to think about what this is yet.

All I can do is look at the river.

"So, I'm gone." Jonathan looks at me. "Which is kind of what I meant before."

"When are you going?"

"Summer. They want me to finish the school year. My dad'll go out now, find a house. My mom and I'll go later."

I kick at the roof. "I'm going to see my dad in June."

He nods. Like that answers something for him.

For a long time we don't say anything. Jonathan says, "Actually, I have an uncle in New Jersey. I was thinking I could stay with him. But my dad said, 'No way.' Apparently I am not to be trusted. Who knew?"

"I would trust you." At first I don't look at him, then I do.

He half smiles. "Yeah, what do you know? You think doors are dangerous."

"I don't anymore."

"You're a girl who thinks she's a guy."

"No. Just if I could choose, that felt . . . freer." I try and make a joke out of it. "You know, in stories it's always like girls are getting someone or losing someone."

Jonathan shrugs. "Guys lose people too."

"I know." I reach out, pull at the lace of my sneaker. "So how does the story end?"

"Which one?"

I think. "Gareth and Evans?"

He smiles. "Oh, they would have kicked ass. Taken over. No question."

"What about the other story?"

"What? After the big seduction scene?" He's staring straight ahead.

"Yeah."

"Oh, I think they would have screwed each other up in all sorts of interesting ways. But I think in the end somebody would've put a stop to it."

"Maybe by that time they wouldn't have let them stop it. Maybe they would have kicked ass and taken over."

He smiles. "Dangerous doors . . ."

"Why?"

"No, man, you live in Fantasy Land."

I think about that for a moment. Sometimes fantasy is stuff that couldn't possibly be true.

But sometimes it's stuff that just isn't true yet. Like going to the moon used to be.

I look down at our shoes. His boots, my sneakers, side by side.

I lace my fingers together, then pull them apart. "You never told me. . . ."

"Told you what?"

"What was the third secret? Remember? Evans's three secrets?"

Jonathan frowns, as if he's thinking. "Can't remember. I think it's the one that was true."

At some point we know it's time. The moment you realize you actually can't stay up here forever is the moment you realize you have to go back.

And that's when you know you may as well go.

Because thinking about it only makes it worse.

I don't think about lasts on the way down.

But when we're standing in the hallway, and all that's left is for me to go through my door and Jonathan to go through his, I have all these questions in my head. Like, Could we write? Before you go, could we do something? I mean, is this honestly the last time I see you?

But I don't ask. Because who knows?

Instead I hug him. And I am hugged. Hard. And for a long time we stay that way. I feel his chin on my hair, the weight of his head on mine.

I think, *This is Jonathan. I know Jonathan.*

And he knows me.

I can't remember the last time I went to the Natural History Museum. Which is weird because it used to be my favorite place in the world. That and the planetarium, which I used to think was way cool. I don't know what I'd think of it now. Probably that it was a goof.

Places you haven't been for a while usually look smaller. But not the museum. It's definitely impressive. I think I'm the only person my age here. Other than me, it's all parents with little kids crazy for dinosaurs.

When you walk into the Hall of Ocean Life, you don't see the blue whale right away. At least, you don't realize that's what you're seeing. It's so massive, hanging from the ceiling, suspended by its tail, like it's diving to the bottom.

Of course, the thing to do is go and walk around underneath it. When I was a kid, I refused to do that because I was convinced it would fall on me. And I still feel that way a bit, wandering around, staring up at the white speckled underbelly, the mouth that stretches for miles, the big old thrashing tail.

I see how Jonathan thought it was real. Because in its own way it is.

I walk around the rest of the exhibit, including the quite cool diorama of the sperm whale battling it out with the giant squid. It's interesting because you're not sure who's winning, and you think, Huh, no matter how big you are, there's still some predator that can get you. It's not just the little guys. Whether you're a shark or a minnow, there's always something bigger.

I walk upstairs to the balcony, where you can stand eye level with the whale. Looking into its yellow eye, which always seems to know you're watching, I think if this were a real whale, it would be dead. It would have been alive in the ocean, and someone would have killed it by shooting a harpoon through its brain or dragging it under and drowning it.

They'd have to stuff it, I guess. Like taxidermy. Take out all the guts, the brain, shoot it up with embalming fluid. It'd be hollow inside, stuffed with emptiness and nothing.

Basically, every time you looked at it, you'd think how someone murdered it so you could see it in a museum. If it were real, you'd think about how it's not supposed to be here, how this is all wrong, like you stole something that didn't belong to you. It'd be a lot of pain.

If something's not real, you're not supposed to care about it. You're supposed to think, Uck, it's fake, who cares?

But not the blue whale. It's so big and so fragile. I wonder who got the idea? Who said, Hey, let's make a life-size blue whale and stick it up on the ceiling? It seems totally crazy, but it works. Yeah, it's all fiberglass and paint. But every time I see it, I feel how incredible and rare and precious these creatures are, how you have to protect them.

I guess someday I'll see the real thing.

But still. This was pretty amazing.

TWENTY-TWO

If you had asked me last year what I would be doing during finals week, I probably would have said

1. Studying my butt off
2. Freaking out
3. Helping Leia Taplow study and freak out

I definitely, no way in a million years, would have said, "Oh, I'll be hanging around Ms. Isaacs's classroom waiting for Katie Mitchell to finish her math final. And I'll be really worried about whether she passes, because if she doesn't, she won't be here next year, which would suck."

And yet, both of those are true. It's almost three thirty, and I'm sitting on the hallway floor waiting for Katie to come out and tell me she did absolutely great, no problem.

I so want her to do well. It'll be monstrously unfair if she doesn't. She's worked so hard.

Nobody else is around. Everyone's either taking tests or, if they're done, long gone. A lot of kids make plans to meet after finals. In diners or the park or whatever. I told Katie we could go to whatever restaurant she wants, as long as they let me wear jeans and sneakers.

A lot of people have already finished the exam. I don't think there can be too many people left in Ms. Isaacs's classroom.

Except for Katie. And maybe a few others.

Okay, so she wasn't one of the first people to finish. Doesn't mean anything. I wasn't the first to finish any of my tests, but I still think I did okay.

Kayla Hartman and Peter Dunphy come out. As they close the door behind them they're completely silent. Then the second it closes, they burst out talking. . . .

"Oh, my God . . ."

"That *sucked*."

"God, could you believe what she put on there?"

"Some of those things, I know we never studied."

As they pass by I say, "Hey, guys."

They stop, look at me like, *Okay, you're here—why?*

"How'd it go?"

"Uh . . ." Kayla grins. "Not too bad." She looks at Peter, who says, "Yeah, not too horrendously dire."

"Is Katie still in there?"

"Yeah." They both make sympathy faces.

"Thanks."

Kayla smiles. "Yeah, no problem."

They start walking away. Then Kayla calls over her shoulder, "Have a great summer."

Which startles me, so I don't answer right away. Then I remember the right words and say, "Hey, yeah, you too. Really."

Then, "See you next year."

Then the door opens again, and I look up, expecting to see Katie. And all of a sudden I'm looking Leia Taplow right in the eye.

She looks as startled as I feel.

Then she just ducks her head and turns around. Like, *I am out of here.*

I call out, "Hey, Leia."

She stops.

To her back I say, "This is dumb, you know. It's lame."

Now she's looking at me at least.

"So why don't we stop it?"

"Stop what?" She looks at me all wide eyed, like we have no problem at all.

Which pisses me off.

I say, "Look, if you want to pretend that we were never friends, that you didn't totally dump me and haven't been

243

spreading my business all over school, fine. But that's not what happened, and we both know it."

Now she drops the "I have no clue" routine. She's got her hands on her hips, and her eyes are hard. "Oh, you think you know what really happened."

Here we go. She's going to make this all about the phone calls. That would have scared me a few months ago; a few months ago I would have backed right down.

But not now.

I say, "I'm sorry I annoyed you—"

Leia interrupts. "You didn't annoy me." I try to answer, but she shouts, "You didn't annoy me, you freaked me out."

"Okay, I'm sorry." I try to sound as calm as possible.

"You were calling me all the time."

"Well, maybe if you had ever picked up the phone, I wouldn't have."

"I mean, God, my mother was like, 'Who is this girl?'"

There's something whiny and scared about the way Leia mentions her mom that makes me feel strong enough to say, "I don't know, Leia. Maybe your friend?"

"Yeah, well, friends don't stalk you."

"Yeah, and friends don't dump you either without explaining why." Then before she can say anything, I go on. "I'm sorry. I thought we were friends, and I didn't want that to stop."

She doesn't say anything to that for a moment. Then she blurts out, "It's not like I didn't want to be friends, I just thought we weren't anymore."

I nod.

"You were so angry all the time. I felt like I didn't know you. Like the littlest thing pissed you off."

I'm about to say, "Like what?" But then I remember Kevin Weymouth. Being obnoxious in the restaurant.

Leia says, "I guess when you called, I didn't pick up because I was scared about what you'd say. Like you'd scream at me or something."

"Yeah, right, 'cause I'm such this big screamer."

"Well, I don't know." Leia looks down at her feet. "That's how it felt."

How this feels to me is like a big fat cop-out. And part of me would really like to let Leia have it. Because this is what she always does, acts all weak and scared so no one feels like they can ever hurt her or say mean things. . . .

But a bigger part of me wants to stop being mad at her. Basically, I don't want her to matter anymore.

"I would never have screamed at you," I tell her. "But I'm sorry if I flipped you out. I wasn't at my most sane."

Leia looks at me. "Why? What was happening?"

It's not mean, the way she asks, and for a second I feel like explaining to her the whole thing about Seventy-first Street. I wonder if I'd told her all that time ago, if maybe we'd be friends now.

But the fact is I didn't, and we're not, and I don't think I want to tell someone who's not my friend about that. So I just say, "Lot of stuff."

Then because I don't want to talk about anything real, I ask, "So, how's old Kevin Weymouth?"

She laughs. "Ugh, please, don't remind me."

"What? I thought you were so nuts for him."

She grins. "Yeah, hello, moved on?"

I grin back. "Yeah, weird how that happens."

She rolls her eyes, but she gets what I'm saying. And for two seconds it's almost like we're friends again.

Only we're not. Which is strange, to know that someone you once really, really cared about is going to be a stranger you pass by in the hallway. Like, maybe you say hi.

What's even stranger is that it's okay.

"So, can we . . . live in peace?" I make a little peace sign.

She laughs. "Yeah, I guess."

"Cool."

You feel like you should say something. "Well, sorry we're not friends anymore. Bye."

Then Leia says, "I am sorry about those guys hassling you. If I think about it, I maybe said some wacko stuff to them."

I don't say anything. Because I can tell Leia does sort of think I'm madly in love with her. Or at least that I was. I'd love to say to her, "You're actually not my type," or something like that. But since I have no idea what my type is, I won't.

I do know Leia isn't it, however.

"Are you going . . ." She points toward the stairs.

"Nah, I'm waiting for Katie to finish."

"Oh." She nods. "Well, take care."

"Yeah, you too."

I turn to look out the window. And when I look back, she's gone.

A few minutes later Katie comes barreling out into the hallway.

"Can't speak. Must have . . . chocolate in large quantities."

So we go to Serendipity's.

Katie doesn't say a word as we order our frozen hot chocolates. She just sits there and sighs deeply. At one point she even swoons sideways, like she's fainted.

Finally I say, "Was it that bad?"

Katie shudders. "Awful. The worst."

I try not to show how disappointed I feel. I feel awful for Katie because she worked so hard. And awful for me, too, frankly.

Then I hear her say, "I think I did okay, though."

I look at her; she's got this grin on her face. I tell her, "You're a megacreep, you know that."

Katie laughs. "Sorry, had to. You were way too serious." She pulls a face like *The Scream,* hands on the sides of her face.

"When do you know for sure?"

"Ms. Isaacs said she would call when she was done grading them. That way I don't have to wait until we get our grades in the mail."

"That's cool of her."

"Yeah, she's okay. I mean, not you, but okay."

I smile, shrug a little. It's the only thing you can do when people compliment you.

"Would you stop it? I mean it. Thank you." She points her straw at me to show she's serious.

I point my straw back. "Well, thank you. For staying."

"No, thank yoouu."

"No, thank yoooouuuu." People are starting to look at us weirdly, so we stop.

"So, wow." Katie crosses her eyes over her hot chocolate. "Wild year, huh?"

I think about it. "Yeah. It was."

"Can't believe it's almost over." She leans down, slurps from her straw. "What are you doing for summer?"

"Uh, in a week or two I'm going to see my dad. For a month. He's in Seattle."

"Is that gruesome or okay?"

I shrug. "Gruesome and okay? What about you?"

"Oh, there's this whole itinerary." She rolls her eyes. "But hey—let's . . . you know."

"Stay in touch." I grin.

"Yeah, stupid! Like, call me."

"Okay."

"Like . . . this weekend."

I laugh. "Okay."

By the time I get home, my mom's already there. I hear her talking as I come through the door, and think, Weird. Who's here? Then I see she's on the phone. She smiles, waves.

Then she says, "Yeah, Bill, as a matter of fact, she just walked in the door."

I mouth, "Dad?" and she nods.

Okay. Bizarre. How long have they been talking on the phone? They never talk to each other. It's always like, "Hi, here's the kid."

"Um-hm. And I think you should discuss this with her." She looks at me like, *Yes, you are "her."* "Well, see what she says."

She holds out the phone to me. As I take it I want to ask, "Discuss what?" But the line's open and my dad would hear. So I just put it to my ear and say, "Hey, Dad."

"Judith, hi. How are you, sweetheart?"

"Good," I say.

I glance at my mom, but she says, "I'll get out of your way," and leaves.

"So," I say. "How are you?"

"Well, I'm thinking," says my dad.

"Oh, yeah? About what?"

"I'm thinking about this summer. I'm thinking I'd really like to see you."

"Well, you will," I say. "In, like, a week or two."

"No, I'm thinking . . . I'm hoping that maybe instead of a month, you'd like to come out for longer. Maybe even the whole summer."

The whole summer? That's like forever.

I don't know what to say. My dad is sounding all intense, like this is important to him.

I look back to where my mom was standing. And all of

a sudden I figure it out, what this is really about: 158 West Seventy-first Street. Jonathan. Get the kid out of the evil danger zone.

I sigh. "You don't have to do this, Dad."

"I don't have to what?"

"You don't have to do this because of what Mom told you. About what happened. It's okay. I'm okay."

Now there is a long, long pause. So long that I wonder if we got disconnected.

Into the phone I say, "Hello?"

"Yeah, I'm here," my dad says. Then in a funny, tight voice he says, "I'm not sure what you're talking about, sweetheart. What happened?"

My heart goes completely still. My dad sounds so uncertain, like he's scared of what I'll say, but he really wants me to say it anyway.

Maybe that's why I can't say anything.

"See," my dad says, "that's the thing, Judith. I don't know what happened, I don't know what's happening with you. I feel like when we talk, it's the same things over and over, and I feel like I'm losing you a bit, sweetheart. That's why I'm hoping you'll come out for the summer. I thought we could do some hiking. . . . Anyway, look, it doesn't matter what we do. I'd just like to see you. You know, you're not here, and I'm not there, and I miss you."

"I miss you, too." That's like tears; I can't stop it, it just comes out.

For a while neither of us says anything. Which is kind of good.

Then my dad says, "So, you'll think about it?"

"I will give it my serious consideration."

"Good." He laughs. "That's all I can ask. So—what is going on?"

I'm about to say, "Finals, school, you know." But then I stop.

And I actually tell him. About everything. Including Jonathan.

"That sounds really tough," he says.

"Yeah. But sort of great, too. Does that make sense?"

"Completely."

"Dad?"

"Yeah?"

I want to ask: "What do you do when things change and it sucks, but there's nothing you can do about it? What do you do when you miss someone?"

Because for the first time I think maybe he would know.

TWENTY-THREE

The night before I leave for Seattle, I ask my mom, "What are you going to do?"

She's helping me pack. Or she thinks she's helping me. What she's really doing is telling me how I packed all the wrong things.

But it's okay. She's letting me go, and that's what's important.

Now she's got an armful of long-sleeve shirts she's trying to find room for. "What do you mean?"

"For the summer. I mean, you're going to be, like, totally free."

She laughs shortly. *Yeah, right.* But she doesn't look so focused on the suitcase anymore.

"I don't know," she says slowly. "I hadn't thought about it."

"Well, you should."

"I guess I should."

She puts three long-sleeve shirts in my suitcase, takes out some stuff, including my notebook. "That has to stay," I tell her.

"Honey . . ." She holds it up. "There are notebooks on the West Coast."

"But I want that one," I say lightly.

She tries a different tack. "You shouldn't be doing work on your vacation."

"It's not work," I tell her. "It's a journal. Dad's going to take me to all these places, and I might see something I want to remember."

She hesitates, then puts it back in the suitcase. Then she picks up *The Making of the Atomic Bomb*. "Surely you can leave this behind. It weighs a ton."

I take it from her and put it back in the case. "Nope, that comes too."

She starts to argue, but I say, "Hey, it's my bag, I'm carrying it, so what do you care?"

My mom shuts her mouth. Handing me the shirts, she says, "Fine. Right. I am now out of this. But don't call me from Seattle when you're cold," she jokes.

"Mom, they have long-sleeve shirts in Seattle."

Flying is a very strange thing. Like all of a sudden you're not where you were, but you're not where you're going, either.

In fact, you're not sure where you are.

I kind of like that.

My mom bought me all these postcards at the airport. I'm supposed to send one to her every day or so. But I figure she won't mind if I use a few for other people.

> Dear Katie,
>
> Clouds. I'm seeing a lot of clouds and eating a lot of pretzels. In four hours I will see my dad. I hope I remember what he looks like. It'll be too strange if we're both walking around the airport going, "Uh, who are you? Do I know you?"
>
> Anyway, I'm really happy you're staying at Connolly. I think next year will be much less insane than this one!

I think for a moment. Then write, "Love, Judith."

I put the card back in my knapsack and pull another one out. But then I put it back and watch cartoons instead.

After I get my bag, I go to the arrivals gate because that's where my dad said to meet. At least, I think he said that's where. Because when I look at the crowd, I don't see anyone I know. I think: Okay, I came to the wrong place entirely.

But then I hear my name and turn around. I walk over

to my dad like, *Yeah, knew it all along.* I'm about to say, "Hi," but he hugs me before I can.

He still smells the same. Which is nice.

My dad's a teacher, so he gets the whole summer off. Sometimes we take a drive, go hiking. We see movies, ride bicycles. He cooks dinner and I help. He's a very good cook, much better than my mom, I must admit.

Every night when I write in my notebook, it seems we haven't done a lot. But it feels like a lot.

One day I ride into town on my bike. I see this café with tables outside, and I decide to sit down and have an iced coffee.

For a few minutes I feel really conspicuous, like I shouldn't be there at all. So I get out my notebook and act like I'm some college student taking notes.

I write:

> I am sitting outside a café. I am drinking a very large iced coffee. I suspect that everyone who walks by looks at me and wonders, Who is that strange girl, and why is she just sitting there drinking coffee?

I look at the street, wondering if I can describe it. A yellow car rolls by, honks at another car. Two women with a baby carriage walk past, talking. The table I'm sitting at wobbles a little.

It's very quiet. There's really nothing dramatic about it at all. There's nowhere you look and think, Ooh, that's weird. What's that? It's all just . . . going on.

Which is also kind of nice.

> Dear Jonathan,
> I am on the other end of the country. Where are you? Have you moved yet?
> I guess if you have, you might not get this. But I hope you do.
> I hope you tell me where you are once you get there.
>
> Judith

Three months later when I get home, my mom gives me a huge hug. Then she says, "Call Katie. That's the first thing I'm supposed to tell you. And tell her I told you to, because she's been worried I'll forget."

I grin. "Okay. What's the second thing?"

"I'm glad you're back."

It feels very strange to be back. My room feels abandoned, like no living thing has disturbed it for eons. For a second I think, I shouldn't have come back, I don't live here anymore.

I'm not sure what to do, so I put my bag on the floor and pick up the phone.

As I dial I think, This could be very weird. What if we have nothing to say to each other?

But the second I hear, "Oh, my God, you're *back*! This is *excellent*!" I think, Yep, definitely back.

To celebrate my coming home, my mom takes us out to dinner. She asks me a million questions: What was it like? What's my dad's house like? Was the weather great?

Finally she says, "It sounds like you had a really wonderful time."

I hesitate. Not because I didn't, but because I did and I don't want to hurt my mom's feelings.

Then she says, "Honey, it's okay if you had a great summer. I didn't have a terrible summer myself."

"Yeah? What'd you do?"

"I caught up with lots of friends. I took some dance classes. . . ." She squeezes my hand. "And a lot of the time I hated it and I missed you. But I told myself that in a few years you're going to be away for a lot longer than just the summer, so hey, I better get used to it."

I think about that. About college, and moving out. About not living with my mom or my dad.

I say, "I don't want to think about that yet."

My mom bursts out laughing. "Good! Me neither!"

There is a new family moving in next door. They're young, with a baby. One time when I'm on my way to see Katie, I run into them and they ask me about schools.

As we stand in the hallway the door to their apartment is open, and I can see inside. It's painted all white and completely empty. You'd never know the Heitmans lived there at all.

Someone scratched over the swastika on the sixth-floor button. They used a key or a knife or something. It doesn't look great, but it's much, much better than it was.

I don't know if it was Jonathan. But I like to think so.

For the first day of school Katie and I meet up a block away so we can go in together. That way you get a little normal time before all the madness starts.

She says, "Hey, I got a new *Sims* program. I'm gonna start fresh. All new characters."

"What ever happened to Clarissa and Nick Nice Guy?"

Katie smiles dreamily. "They met with a terrible accident. . . ."

On the first day you have to sign up for your classes. I'm trying to figure out if Mr. Bennett for "Modern American Lit" is more boring than Ms. Hapshaw for "Poetry Through the Ages," when I feel someone nudge my backpack.

I turn around and see Michael Ruddick and Madelyn Kim. Michael's wearing a shirt that says THE GEEK SHALL INHERIT THE EARTH.

"Hey—are you going to take Jarman this year?" asks Madelyn.

"Um, yeah." I look at their faces, trying to see if this is good news or not. "Am I insane?"

"Probably," says Michael, straight-faced.

Madelyn elbows him. "Us too. Should be a cool group."

"Excellent." I grin. "Hey, on the first day let's ask him if we can blow off class due to good weather."

They laugh. Then they start moving over to the math sign-up table. I half raise my hand to wave bye.

Then I realize they're waiting for me.

I think, Oh, duh, and join them.

After dinner I do some research for a paper that's due Monday. It's only the third week of school, but the pressure's already on. This year, though, I'm determined not to let it freak me out.

In fact, after half an hour I stop and check my e-mail. There's a message from my dad called **Hi! Howareyou?** which makes me laugh. Over the summer we decided that e-mail was much better than the phone.

There's also a message from Katie.

Help! Am about to go on hot date with Bodacious Biker Boy and must choose! Candlelight dinner or romantic walk in the park? Need advice NOW!

I type back, **Why are you walking if the guy's got a bike?**

A second later I get a message. **You're right. Am dumping him and switching to Casanova Sam. He's mad for my form!**

I laugh and am about to type back, "But are you mad for his?" when a new message pops up.

From: Jonathan@connect.com
Subject: I'm Here

For the longest time I just stare at the screen.
I think, Do I dare?
Yes. I do.
Click . . .
. . . open.

Thank you . . .

To Mom, Devon, Stacey, Pearl, Larry, Peggy, John W., Nina, Kristen, Benjamin, and all my friends and relatives who barged into bookstores demanding a copy of *The True Meaning of Cleavage*.

To anyone who ever read *The True Meaning of Cleavage*. You made a dream come true.

To all those book sellers and librarians who were kind enough to take a first novel seriously.

To Virginia Skrelja, for being honest about the early drafts and encouraging about everything else.

To Hilary Goodman, for answering all my stupid questions with such patience.

To Ginee Seo, who has such taste and class.

To the ridiculously talented people at Simon & Schuster who design, sell, copyedit, and do a million other things to make a book work.

To Dana Florin-Weiss, for enlightening me about the macabre side of *Sims*.

To her brother, Josh, who started all of this.

To Sandy, because she's great.

To her daughter, Katherine, who is also great.

To Sam, for her guerilla UK campaign, and everything else.

To Toby Eichas and the kids of J. P. Taravella High School, for turning a rotten morning into one of the nicest days of my life.

To all the people who shared their knowledge of the gaming world. Your identities are safe with me.

And to Jonathan, whose identity is also safe with me.

SIMON AND SCHUSTER

This book and other SIMON AND SCHUSTER Children's titles are available from your local book shop or can be ordered direct from the publisher.

0 6898 3722 4	The True Meaning of Cleavage	Mariah Fredericks	£5.99
0 6898 6065 X	The V Club	Kate Brian	£5.99
1 4169 0126 4	The Ruling Class	Francine Pascal	£5.99

Please send cheque or postal order for the value of the book,
free postage and packaging within the UK, to
SIMON & SCHUSTER CASH SALES
PO Box 29, Douglas, Isle of Man, IM99 1BQ
Credit cards accepted.
Tel: 01624 677237, Fax: 01624 670923
www.bookpost.co.uk

Please allow 14 days for delivery.
Prices and availability subject to change without notice.

THE TRUE MEANING OF CLEAVAGE
by Mariah Fredericks

Sari and Jess are best friends and total opposites. They've liked each other ever since they discovered that they are the only two normal people at Eldridge Alternative. As they prepare to face the trials of year ten, Sari is psyched. Jess, not so much. How can she face the Prada Mafia, the most evil clique at school? Or Mr McGuiness's unnervingly long nose hair?

What if something really interesting happens to Sari and nothing whatsoever to Jess?

Then when Sari falls madly, psychotically in love with David Cole, the coolest and most popular senior, not even Jess can predict the mayhem that is about to start...

ISBN 0 689 83722 4